Totally Bound Publishing books by Destiny Moon:

Amply Rewarded
All I Ever Wanted
Worth the Wait
Perfect on Paper

I0570369

PERFECT ON PAPER

DESTINY MOON

Perfect on Paper
ISBN # 978-1-78430-776-9
©Copyright Destiny Moon 2015
Cover Art by Posh Gosh ©Copyright September 2015
Interior text design by Claire Siemaszkiewicz
Totally Bound Publishing

Published in 2015 by Totally Bound Publishing, Newland House, The Point, Weaver Road, Lincoln, LN6 3QN, United Kingdom.

PERFECT ON PAPER

Dedication

For B.

Chapter One

The only black dress that Nadine owned was the one dress she couldn't wear to her grandfather's funeral. With its white piping trim, it was way too festive, flirty and fun for a funeral. It was a snug-fitting Alfred Sung knee-length dress that she'd bought with the bonus she'd made last year.

Last year.

She didn't dare to even think about what her life had been like then. She forced the memories out of her mind as she drove to Sally's thrift shop. She needed to buy something—anything—black. She'd never wear it again after laying dear Grandpa Winston to rest.

"Nadine," Sally, the shop owner, exclaimed as soon as Nadine inched past the clanging bell that dangled on the glass door. "I heard about dear Winston. I'm so sorry."

With that, Nadine cried into Sally's warm embrace that smelled like Coty perfume from the seventies. Nothing at Sally's had changed in decades, even fragrance. There was solace in that. With that, the tears came.

"I need a dress for…" she sniveled. It was so hard to say the words. All she managed, by way of explanation, was, "Sunday."

Sally gave her an empathetic smile. "I've just the thing, dear."

She went to the rack along the side and pulled a long dress from it. It wasn't something that Nadine would ordinarily wear. She eyed its shapeless form.

"Perfect."

"You should try it on, just to be sure it fits."

Nadine held it to herself. The thing was ugly, that was for sure, but it would definitely fit. It was loose. That was the style. She'd have to cinch it with a belt or something. It didn't much matter. She'd figure it out at home.

"I'll take it."

"But…"

"It's fine. I'll be bringing it back to you next week."

"I know you will, dear. Why don't you just borrow it?"

"No. Let me pay you for it."

"All right then."

Sally went around the counter to the old cash register that had been the same since Nadine had been a kid. She rang up the purchase.

"That'll be three dollars."

Nadine almost cried again. She knew that Sally was discounting the dress by several hundred percent, but she understood why. Her grandfather had also helped Sally many times over the years, offering advice and a helping hand whenever he could. He had done that for everyone in the neighborhood.

She placed a five-dollar bill in the elderly woman's hand. "Will you be there on Sunday?"

"Wouldn't miss it."

They hugged again and Nadine left the store.

On her way home, she picked up a salad from the grocery store and, although it went against her rules, she also grabbed a bottle of merlot. She wasn't one to drink alone, but this was different. She couldn't be around her family. She didn't know how to even begin to add her grandfather's death to the horrid typhoon of events that had turned her life upside down in the past few months. It was better to be alone with her thoughts and feelings until she had a bit of a handle on them.

The past year had changed everything. It had started half a year ago when she'd lost her job at Simmons & Co, where she'd been one of their best investors. It wasn't her fault, her manager had said, just the result of the recent market meltdown. She shouldn't blame herself, she'd been told.

Telling Allan had been hard. All their wedding plans had already been set in motion. Their credit cards had had charges for things like deposits on the church gazebo, tent rentals, chair rentals and a big four-tier butter cream cake. He'd told her they'd get through it together, so she'd leaned on him.

Then there had been that horrible day, a couple of months later — their engagement party — when he'd left her in front of all their friends and relatives. The aunts and cousins and neighborhood ladies had all said it was a simple case of cold feet — that most men got that. But most men did not walk out on relationships they'd been in since high school just because they were a little nervous, Nadine was convinced. Though she had accepted the kinder explanations in the moment, she knew he was gone. Because even if he tried to come back, the memory was too painful for her to overcome. She knew that she could not marry a man who would leave her at their engagement party. There was just no recovering from that.

Nadine ate her salad in front of the evening news, the living room dimmed all around her. The local news did a segment on Winston's Fine Furniture and the role her grandfather had played in the community. It was almost too much to bear.

* * * *

Sunday was cold. Nadine put on the frumpy black dress and made the best of her hair and makeup. She didn't care how she looked. This was a day for crying.

Throughout the service she sniffled, unable to accept that he was actually gone. He'd been so present in her life, the one member of her family who had never hurt her feelings.

After the service, there was tea and cake in the community room adjacent to the chapel. Nadine took a slice of someone's homemade lemon loaf onto a plate.

Her aunt Martha made a face and came over to her. "Careful, dear," she said. "Now that you're single again, you have to watch that figure."

Oh boy.

Was that really what she cared about on a day like today?

"Thanks," Nadine said, taking a bite. "I'm sure it'll be fine."

"You've got your mother's hips. And you know what *that* means."

Nadine scowled. How many times had the mean aunts made fun of her mom's slightly larger than average hips? It was one thing at a birthday celebration, but this was Grandpa Winston's day.

Aunt Shirley sauntered up to them. "I'm not interrupting, am I?"

"No," Nadine said, taking another bite of lemon cake.

"So, tell us," Aunt Shirley said with her usual gregarious smile, "are you seeing anyone yet?"

"No," Nadine said, her tone cool and formal. "Not yet."

"Well, no need to worry, dear. You're young."

What was that supposed to mean? Was it really so hideous in the minds of her aunts to be an unwed woman over thirty? Wasn't it better to be single than to have married the kind of guy who'd walk out?

"I'm keeping busy with work," she said, in an effort to justify her life.

"Oh, yes. That's right. Our little investment broker," Aunt Shirley said, squeezing Nadine's arm.

"Our career girl," Aunt Martha agreed.

"Well, actually, I'm back at the bookstore, remember?" *Does nobody around here ever listen?*

"Heavens, no. I don't think I heard that," Aunt Shirley said.

Nadine wanted to roll her eyes, but there was no point. Her aunts did their best. "Yeah, at the university. It's a decent job with benefits. When Simmons & Co laid me off last year, I had to take it."

"Oh dear." Aunt Martha looked at her with pity. Both of her mother's sisters seemed evil to her in that moment. Their focus shouldn't even be on Nadine's life at all. If there was one time to not have to face their catty gossip, surely it'd be a day like this.

"I still don't believe it's over between you and Allan," Aunt Martha said, as though it was supposed to be a comfort.

"Shirley's right. He'll be back for you."

Ugh. If that happens, I'd rather join Grandpa Winston.

Nadine excused herself and wandered away. She couldn't be around their negative views. She, too, felt that her life had fallen apart. She no longer had her glamorous job. She'd lost the status of having a fiancé, which in her family meant that she was relegated to sitting at the kids' table at family events. And she had just lost the one man who had accepted her unconditionally — Grandpa Winston. There was nothing that seemed certain anymore except for one little thing. Allan was not a prize worth waiting for. It had hurt her bitterly that he'd left, but if he ever came back, she would definitely not marry him. She might throw a wrench or a brick at him, but marriage was *not* an option.

Chapter Two

One year later

Nadine was up at six, as usual. After her morning yoga, she made a mug of tea and sat down to eat breakfast—oatmeal sprinkled with cinnamon and blueberries. She went over her business affirmations, reciting feel-good phrases in an attempt to convince herself that she could do this. Building up a business from scratch was not easy, but neither was any dream worth striving for. Having given up on her earlier dreams of being Allan's wife and her former firm's youngest and brightest, she had spent the past year seeking clarity. It had come in the form of an epiphany. One day, she had realized that the one thing in this life that made her happy was working with furniture. She'd been happy in all the years of her childhood and adolescence when she'd hung out at Grandpa Winston's shop, watching him for hours at a time as he sanded and varnished. She loved the smell of the solvents he used. And she lived for the scent of wood. It was divine.

As she took a sip of her morning tea, she thought about how strange life was that in all the years when she could have apprenticed with her grandfather, she had never considered it. Now that he was gone, she wanted nothing more than to get back into his workshop and learn from the best. He'd been like a wizard with his hands, working his magic on pieces of furniture that other people had abandoned. It had been incredible to see what he could do with chests of drawers that had survived fires, wars, divorces and years of being locked away in damp garages. Nadine admired not just the beauty he had been able to create, but also the way he saw craftsmanship as something sacred—like he owed it to history and posterity to preserve each and every cabinet and bookshelf and credenza that came his way.

Yet, for all her admiration, Nadine's vision seemed insurmountable this morning. She browsed through the classified section, as she did each morning, looking for a space that might function as a storefront as well as a workshop. She wanted exactly the kind of setup that Grandpa Winston'd had. How she kicked herself for not knowing this a year earlier when her parents had put his very shop up for sale. Grandpa Winston had lived upstairs, done his work in the back and served customers up front for as long as she could remember. Alas, she would have to find some other way to have a storefront. And on a day like this one, it all seemed a little too daunting. In her mind's eye, she saw herself unable to hoist furniture onto the back of her truck. How had her grandfather managed to do it into his golden years? She imagined herself falling into debt, the way so many businesses in this town did. It was quite common in this economy to open a shop and close it down again within the same year for lack of business.

Ann Arbor had suffered just like every other small town across America, and Nadine was afraid. What made her think she could handle it?

She said her affirmations out loud to try to silence the negative thoughts that played continually as the music of her mind.

"I am capable. I am strong. I am successful."

She got up from the breakfast table, put her bowl and mug in the dishwasher, got dressed and did her makeup. By seven, she was in her car. By half past seven, she was at her desk in the basement of the University of Michigan's bookstore. This was busy season—September. This was the time to sock away savings so that when the perfect location became available, she would be able to make her move. She wanted badly to quit this asinine job, but living without medical insurance and a high enough income to support herself? She would not. Her parents had raised her to have high expectations. She was used to the best. But this last year had seen her evaluate what that meant. Nadine had stopped going for regular manicures and pedicures. She'd quit shopping for brand name clothing and expensive cosmetics and fragrances. She'd laid off the cocktail lounges and nice dinners with friends. Everything was about her new dream.

She logged onto the bookstore network and got to work immediately, recording the sales from the night before, inputting orders to textbook suppliers and following up on invoices. Morning was the only time to do this, for once nine o'clock rolled around, she had to supervise the student workforce and make sure they didn't screw up. They had to keep the stock flowing from the skids here in Shipping and Receiving to the stacks on the floor. That was not easy. She remembered it from the other perspective, too, back when she'd been a UMich student and this had been her part-time job. But now she was the boss, and she vowed to do the best she could.

After all, if everything went her way, this would be the last job she ever had. If she could secure a deposit on a storefront, she'd take a chance on the only dream that mattered. And she'd call it Nadine's Fine Furniture, in the tradition of her grandfather.

Chapter Three

David went to the staffroom to put away his coat and book bag. The lockers were all full already, so he put his stuff down in a corner beside the kitchenette.

"Not there," a muffled voice said.

David turned to see a guy cramming the last bite of a sandwich into his face.

"It's a fire hazard."

"How's it a fire hazard?"

"Beats me, dude," the guy said, still chewing. "Just sayin'."

"Well, where should I put this?" David had his arms full.

The guy shoved a pile of coats to one side as if his forearm was a wedge. He made a crevice that barely looked like it could fit a handbag and gestured for David to hand his stuff to him.

"Here's some space."

"Thanks, man," David said, checking himself in the staffroom mirror. Nothing in his teeth, so that was good. But he could've combed his hair. *Oh well.*

The guy was being nice. "Don't worry about it. It's your first day, right? I wouldn't want to see you start off on the wrong foot with Nadine."

"Who's she? I've only met Hank."

"Yeah, Hank's upstairs where it's civilized. Nadine is the goddess of the underworld."

"Huh?" David was skeptical.

"She manages Shipping and Receiving and everything on the textbook floor, and there's nothing she hates more than us part-timers getting in her way. Anyway, your backpack will be fine here. Let's get upstairs."

David followed the guy through a maze of textbooks to a giant staircase and up to the main floor of the university bookstore.

A crowd of other clipboard-toting trainees clustered around Hank, who was not yet in training mode. Actually, it looked like he was flirting with a couple of the girls, but who could tell?

* * * *

After the first training session, David's mind was in overload. There were so many transactions to remember. Being a cashier was a lot more complicated than he had thought it would be, but the job was a major score. Every undergrad wanted to work at the bookstore. The union wages were high and access to advance purchasing and jumping the line-ups were perks that made all the difference in the first week of classes. Besides, after six months of living on an island off the coast of Cuba with his old friend from elementary school, David felt like the job was a great way to get back into the capitalist disciplined schedule he'd tried to rebel against while surfing and lying on the beach watching the pelicans fly by.

Hank dismissed the trainees after only two hours. "Consider it a bonus," he said. "You'll all be paid for four hours."

Everyone cheered. One of the two girls Hank had flirted with earlier said—a little too loudly—"Oh my God. Hank is so nice." She giggled and led the group of trainees downstairs. As David made his way to the staircase, a guy came up beside him.

"First year at the bookstore?" he asked.

"Yeah. You?"

"Nah. Third year. Best job on campus."

"Tell me about it. I'm going to try to hang onto this gig for the rest of my degree."

"You and everyone else here. I'm Sam." He extended his hand, a gesture David didn't see often. He shook it.

"David."

"Word of advice, though. If anyone asks you to trade a cashiering shift for one in Shipping and Receiving, don't do it."

"Why not?"

"Just trust me."

As they made their way to the staffroom, David caught a glimpse of a buxom blonde—likely a professor considering her gray pencil skirt and fitted, silky coral blouse.

"Shit, that's her. Look down," the guy said.

"Who?"

"Nadine," he whispered then he made a beeline for the staffroom. "Goddess of the underworld."

She was surveying a complex floor stack of textbooks, stepping back and analyzing it as though it was a sculpture at an art museum. David's jaw dropped. She did look like a goddess, but not one who reigned over an ancient hell. She was stunning.

* * * *

During his first training shift when he was to finally get in front of the register, he worked alongside Chrissy, a pretty kinesiology major with a ski-jump nose. Right after the fifteen-minute break, Hank took her aside for a few minutes. When she got back, she looked upset, but David had a waiting line and so did she, so there was no way to discuss it.

As soon as Hank had closed the front gate on the last student and the bookstore was officially empty and closed, everyone cashed out. A symphony of registers spewed their till tape. It took two minutes, just long enough for Chrissy to tell David what had happened.

She shook her head like she'd been told she had to eat dirt. "Hank wants to take me off cash and put me down in Shipping and Receiving."

David, who hated seeing girls suffer, said, "Could be a nice change of scenery." He shrugged his shoulders, and Chrissy couldn't help but smile.

"He's preying on my niceness and my inability to say no. I'm gonna get eaten alive by the queen of the underworld."

"I believe her official title is goddess of the underworld." David was surprised that Chrissy didn't laugh at his joke.

"She scares me."

David thought for a moment. "Wanna trade?"

"Seriously?" She looked like she was about to hug him.

"Sure."

"Oh my God." She bounced up and down in front of him then flirtatiously wrapped her arms around him for a brief second. "Thank you so much."

She ran off to get Hank to make it official.

They took their registers downstairs to count the cash. Hank found him in the middle of his quarters. He lost count. Hank told him to report to Nadine the following day. David nodded and resumed counting. Had he just made the biggest mistake of the semester?

* * * *

The next morning, after showering with his sandalwood soap, he toweled off and put his hair into a ponytail. It might be time to cut it soon, he thought as he saw himself in the mirror, but it was still only September and he wanted to keep the hair as a reminder of his totally relaxed spring and summer.

He put on his best work clothes—khaki pants and a plaid shirt. Everything about David was casual. His wardrobe mirrored his attitude toward life, and he liked it that way. He got to the bookstore early and was already designing stack layouts in his mind when Nadine came to open the door to the underworld.

"Good morning," he said.

"I thought Hank was giving me that sweet-looking blonde."

"We switched."

"Oh, really?" Nadine's eyes narrowed momentarily. "She asked you to?"

"I offered."

"I see." She turned the key and barged through the thick laminate door. "Well, there's a lot to do, so come with me."

David followed his new boss, careful not to make it obvious that he was checking her out. He couldn't help himself. With her slender shoulders and full hair, she could have been a model. Nadine stopped at a table.

Next to it was a skid, wrapped in plastic cling wrap from top to bottom, like a giant textbook cocoon.

"These are mostly science texts, but pay attention because there could be some business admin books, too. I need them all counted and priced. Then cross reference the paperwork that came with them with the original order and make sure the numbers all line up—so your tallying skills are really important here."

"I'm good at counting," David said. Nadine was clearly not amused.

"Here's your pricing gun." She passed him the plastic contraption. "If you can't figure out how to work it, just ask."

Perhaps it was the way she'd said it, as though he really wouldn't be able to understand the high technology of the pricing gun, but David was determined not to ask for help.

"All right," he answered, as he rolled up his plaid sleeves.

"I'll be at my desk," Nadine said as she walked the eight paces to where she'd be spending her workday and sat down. She faced him. It was undoubtedly the floor layout that made the part-time students give her the nickname. It was nearly impossible not to feel scrutinized and observed like a lab mouse in a tiny cage in front of Nadine. But he was much more creative. He was in her dungeon and her office chair was her throne. He was a lowly peasant boy whose greatest aspiration was to please his queen. *Where did he get this stuff?* He found an X-ACTO knife and freed the skid of books from their plastic encasing. With acute focus, he went through box after box, like an athlete training for the Olympics.

Chapter Four

Nadine sat at her desk and made calls to distributors while she click-clacked away on her keyboard, never once stopping to stare out of the window or swivel in her chair. She did notice David's hard work—it was impossible not to—but she was busy thinking about obstacles of her own. Her mom had just emailed her and even though Nadine would never admit it, she did routinely check her personal email on work time. It was one of the few luxuries she had carried over from the years when she had her own office. Her mom had thrown a wrench into Nadine's weekend plans, and she brainstormed practical ways to avoid letting her mom pull her strings. She'd read enough books by now to avoid being susceptible to the old tactics. She did not want to spend the weekend fawning over her brother Bruce's second baby while her sister-in-law smugly talked about their nanny, recent renovations and the people at the country club. Nadine had plans of her own, dreams of her own. She was so tired of playing second fiddle in the family.

She was jolted back to reality by David, who approached her desk after what seemed like barely an hour.

"Done," he announced.

"Already?"

"I'm fast." He beamed at her. She found it eerie.

"Well, around here, haste usually makes waste, so let's see that paperwork."

He handed her the sheets he'd marked up with tallies. She perused the papers, looking intently for errors. She found none.

"Did you take a break yet?"

"No."

"Do that," she ordered. "When you come back, you can shelve the texts then, after that, I've got another project for you."

* * * *

"See you when you get here." Nadine hung up the phone.

She had confirmed her after-work jog with her best friend Marnie, who worked from home on Tuesdays. One of the challenges of working these hours was that she couldn't run with Marnie like they used to, but on Tuesdays they had a standing date. Nadine had her running gear in her work bag.

Marnie showed up fifteen minutes before Nadine was officially supposed to clock out. Leaving early was not the sort of thing she did, even though the work of the day was accomplished.

"Come in." Nadine brought her friend through the back where they received deliveries.

"Whoa," Marnie said as she entered the basement of the bookstore where Nadine spent forty hours every week. "It's so different from your old office."

A year and a half ago, Marnie wouldn't have dared to come to Nadine's workplace in running gear. Her office had been in the corporate district. Nadine had observed a strict dress code. The lobby of the office tower was reminiscent of five-star hotels, decorated with a huge new bouquet every week and packed with security. The bookstore was the kind of place where employees were allowed to show up in sweatpants if they wanted. Of course, Nadine did not. But it was true what her best friend had observed. Her life had changed so drastically.

"Yeah, grab a chair," Nadine said quietly. She could send a couple more work emails before calling it a day. But her best friend was up to no good, sitting beside her. It was like they were back in high school, with Marnie cracking a quiet joke about the teacher. Nadine was completely distracted.

"Who's the sex god?" she whispered, as soon as David was out of earshot.

"That's David," Nadine said in a proper and professional tone through her clenched teeth. "He's off limits."

Marnie made an exaggerated sad face at the admonishment. "But why?"

"He's young. He's a student. He works for me." Nadine listed off on her fingers. "Want me to keep going?"

"But he's so cute."

"Let him work, Marnie," Nadine scolded. "And behave yourself. Here, read this." Nadine tossed Marnie a book, but they both knew she wasn't going to open Darwin's *On the Origin of Species* for any light reading. However, she took the hint and quietly kept to herself for a little, so Nadine felt that the objective had been accomplished and she could finish her task list.

At three o'clock, David approached Nadine's desk. "Is there anything else?"

"Did you finish the skid?"

"I did. All the textbooks are on the floor, in stacks or on the shelves."

"That's all, then. See you tomorrow."

"All right. See ya." He turned to leave.

He wasn't even out of the swinging doors to the store before Marnie playfully punched Nadine in the arm, so hard that Nadine felt accosted.

"What?"

"What do you mean 'what'? Didn't you see the way he looked at you?"

"David?"

"Yeah, David. He has the hots for you so bad."

"You're making it up. Knock it off."

But Marnie shook her head. "He's in love with you. It's clear as day."

"Marnie, quit it. I'll go change."

Nadine re-emerged from the washroom wearing her running gear — her tight black pants and pink fitted hoodie with matching pink runners.

"Did you see the boy toy out there — or, rather, did he see you?"

"No," Nadine said, "and I don't want you calling him that. It's not appropriate."

"Oooh." Marnie put her hands up in mock defense. "Inappropriate." She mocked Nadine's tone like only a best friend could.

Nadine rolled her eyes. "Come on. Let's run."

They left through the back door.

"You don't really think that David has a little crush, do you?" she asked, as they did pre-run stretches in the cool afternoon air.

"You are so clueless, Nadine." Marnie shook her head.

Chapter Five

Nadine swiveled around on her chair. There was a pile of papers on her desk and she'd promised herself that they'd be dealt with by the end of the week. In order for that to happen, she had to accomplish a lot in a day. She'd broken down her productivity into one-hour goals. This next hour involved clearing out some of the inventory from the storage area. Last year's textbooks that hadn't gone back to publishers, used books and returns all took up a ton of space in storage and there was no chance of students buying what they couldn't see. Logic had it that if she could get the old stock out on the shelves, she'd expose it to customers then her sales levels would go up and that meant she'd have a better chance at the bonus that was so close she could almost see the dollars in her bank account. And boy did she want those dollars. They'd put her closer to her ultimate goal, and this was the year that everything was going to turn around for her. It was all about steady and constant focus. Working the students as hard as she could and as hard as she worked herself.

This David fellow seemed like the kind of guy who could handle her vision.

"I have a task for you," she said.

"Sure. Anything."

"Come with me." She got up out of her chair and flattened the creases in her pencil skirt.

David followed her.

"Where are you taking me?" he asked in a joking voice as they walked through two double doors out into the receiving area. "I've never seen this part of the building before."

"The freight elevator," Nadine said.

"There's a freight elevator?"

"Are you surprised?"

"I had no idea."

"It's an old building. It's been renovated a lot, but there's still this old storage space down in the basement."

"Whoa."

"Yeah, and your task for the next few days will be to clear it out and get all of the stock down there priced and onto the shelves."

"Okay."

She pressed the button with the downward pointing arrow. It lit up. A few seconds later, there was a rumbling sound of the elevator reaching their floor. The elevator doors opened from a horizontal crack down the middle. They stepped in. Nadine yanked on a rope at the top that pulled the top half of the door down and the bottom half up. David looked intently at the process.

"Have you ever been in a freight elevator before?" she asked.

"No."

"Then you're in for a treat. Pretty weird in here, huh?" Nadine didn't ordinarily make small talk with the students but then again, she rarely put herself in a situation wherein small talk seemed appropriate. Usually, she merely delegated from her desk and got back to work. This task required a little more of her.

Instead of buttons on the inside, there was a lever that she held down. She set it to 'Basement'. There was another rumble and they were off.

"Whoa. Neat," David uttered. He sounded excited, as though he was on some kind of strange ride at an amusement park.

Just then another rumbling came and some bouncing then it felt like their downward motion had stopped. The floor of the elevator lift bobbed up and down a little then it was still.

"Don't worry," Nadine said. "This thing never gets stuck."

"I'm not worried," David said.

Nadine had reassured him as a form of projection. She was the one who feared small, enclosed spaces. She hadn't liked them ever since she was a child. One time she got stuck in her grandfather's tool shed out behind his shop. Another time, her brother locked her in the furnace closet and went out to play and several hours passed before anyone came home. In the end, it was her father who found her, balling her eyes out, in wet pants that had dried again, but smelled bad. Her brother was punished, but not enough in Nadine's view. She still secretly resented him for scarring her for life.

"It's okay," Nadine said. "We'll get out."

"Of course we will," David replied.

"I just need to pull on this rope here," she said, trying to open the doors. We might be between floors and we might need to crawl out, but it'll be better than waiting for someone to come.

She heaved with all her might but nothing happened.

"It's supposed to open no matter where we are," she protested.

David grabbed the rope from her. "Here," he said. "Let me."

He pulled hard — the sweat on his brow indicated it was as hard as he could — but nothing seemed to budge.

"Press the emergency button," Nadine said.

David pushed it and it lit up. "Oh good," he said. "It works. We'll be out of here in no time."

Nadine searched her pockets. "I knew I should have brought my cell phone." She shook her head, making it obvious that she was mad at herself for the oversight. "Do you have yours?"

"No. It's in the employee room in my backpack."

"Crap. What if no one got the emergency signal?"

"They did."

"You don't know that." She set the lever to their floor — Receiving — and the floor wobbled again but the elevator didn't go up. "We're really stuck."

"It's okay," David said.

"I can't believe this is happening."

"It's okay," David repeated. "They'll get us out. It won't be long."

"How do you know? You don't know." Nadine fought back the urge to cry. She couldn't afford to lose her cool in front of a student.

She hit the emergency button again and, unlike David, she held it in. There was a ringing sound, like they were phoning a security desk somewhere.

"See?" she admonished. "They didn't get our call before. They have to answer."

"They're getting our call now," David said in a controlled tone. He spoke slowly and calmly as though he wanted to put her at ease.

The phone rang and rang. Four rings then five.

"No one's there," Nadine said, sounding panicked.

"Someone will answer. Give it a second."

"No one's there. No one's coming. We're stuck." Nadine's voice cracked as she spoke.

David took charge of the situation. "Here. Let me." He took her finger off the button and pushed it.

"That's not helping. I was doing it right, but there's *no one* there," Nadine yelled at him.

"Shhh," David said quietly. "No need to raise your voice or worry. We'll get out."

"Easy for you to say." There were tears in her eyes. "I have to tell you something."

"What?"

"I didn't follow procedure."

She kicked the wall of the elevator with her lacquered high-heeled foot. "Ugh! The one time I deviate," she said to herself.

"What do you mean?"

"I'm supposed to tell Hank every time we use the freight elevator."

"So, why didn't you?" David asked. It was the first time she had heard concern in his voice.

"I just wanted to get this done. I didn't want to get slowed down by having to go find him and go through all the rigmarole. It's never been stuck before."

"Um, so, hold on. If it's procedure to tell Hank, and there's no one on the other end of the security line, then that means we're down here but no one knows we're here."

"We're gonna die." Nadine burst into tears. "They'll find us curled up in fetal positions, starved to death — or suffocated. Oh God. What's worse?"

David put his arms around her and let her cry it out. He held onto her and patted her back. He repeated, "We're not going to die. We're not going to die."

Nadine's fears seized her. She relived her childhood trauma all over again, just as she had on carnival rides or that time her friends took her hiking and they went into a cave. Small spaces caused her to panic.

"Help! Help!" they both yelled at the tops of their lungs. It was the only plan that made sense. But no one answered their calls, and after a few minutes they grew tired. Nadine started to cry again.

When the sobbing stage wore off, Nadine got angry. She berated herself internally first. *How could I have been so stupid?* But then her anger turned outward.

"What the hell kind of crappy building is this, anyway?" she called out.

Finally, she'd had enough and couldn't hold her temper in any longer. She flung off her heels and kicked the side of the elevator with all her might. The ball of her foot ached.

That did it. The floor wobbled and the little box they'd been in shook back and forth a little and finally began an upward ascent, letting out a screeching sound.

"You saved us," David said, sounding his usual chipper self again.

They stopped with a thud. Nadine pulled the rope and, this time, the doors came apart quite effortlessly and revealed that they were a mere step away from freedom. It was about two feet up to the floor. David leaped out of the elevator and turned around to offer Nadine a hand.

"Thanks," Nadine said, taking his hand and heaving herself up out of the deathtrap that she vowed here and now never to set foot in again.

Once on the outside, she hugged him again. There came more tears against her will. They were tears of relief.

"I must look a total mess," she said.

"No," he replied. "You made it through and that's the important part. And, hey, you saved us. If you hadn't kicked the side so aggressively, we'd still be in there."

"I got us into the situation. I can't take any credit for getting us out. I'm sorry. I'll never stray from procedure again."

"Well, I'm not going to keep you to that. Life is about straying from procedure."

"Not for me, it isn't. I've learned my lesson."

"So, you don't want to go down to the basement anymore? What about the stock down there?"

"There are better ways of getting a bonus. Let's go back inside."

They walked through the double doors and Nadine promptly took her seat again and opened her drawer, got out a mirror and examined herself.

"Oh my God," she exclaimed. "Frightening." She was red in the face, her eye makeup had smeared and there were dark stains streaking down her cheeks.

"You got scared. Could happen to anyone."

"I wasn't scared. It was a panic attack. There's a big difference."

"Okay," David conceded.

"There is," Nadine insisted defensively. She tensed up again. She went from being a discombobulated mess to resuming her collected demeanor. There was a compact mirror in her top desk drawer that she used to get herself together. Once she had fixed her makeup stains, she dug through her purse, found some mascara and applied it.

She looked up from her desk and caught him watching her. *Why is he looking at me like that?*

"What?" she asked.

"Nothing." He shook his head. David smiled. "So, I guess it's time to get back to work now."

"Well, yeah. Still a couple more hours left before quitting time."

"Nadine, I think you're in shock."

"I am not."

"You are. You don't realize it because you're obviously under a lot of stress, but you're in shock. You might want to call it quits early today."

"No."

"No?" He approached her desk. "Ten minutes ago, you thought you were experiencing the last precious minutes of your life. You can't tell me that you're eager to get back to whatever it is you do at your desk."

"Work, David," she said in a condescending tone. "It's called work."

"Okay," he said with a tone of absolute non-belief. "If you say so."

"I have to get my bonus this year. It's the only possibility. I can't settle for anything less."

"All right. I'm not arguing. Back to work it is."

David took up the price gun and began to lay out more textbooks.

* * * *

A little before the afternoon shift was over, David approached Nadine's desk. She was so engrossed in the spreadsheet she had on her computer screen that she jumped when he entered into her peripheral vision.

"Shhh," he said. "It's okay."

"You could have me fired for endangering you and not following procedure."

"I'd never do that. Don't stress out."

"Is it that noticeable that I'm a total stress case?"

"Probably not to others," he said, trying to put her at ease. "But I saw you face your own mortality this afternoon, so you can't fool me."

Nadine looked directly into his eyes.

"Sometimes I feel like I don't know what I'm doing." Her delivery was simple, as though she was merely stating fact.

"Anything I can help with? I did used to deal with distributors in the past." He motioned to her computer. He would do anything to be useful to her.

"It's not work," she admitted. As though she was thinking it out loud for the first time, she said, "Sometimes I don't know why I'm here."

"At the bookstore? Or on planet Earth? Work problem? Or existential crisis?" This was the moment he'd been waiting for, a chance to get to know the vulnerable part of her that she kept behind her brave veneer.

"It's not the job," she said. "Well, it is. But that's not all. Do you ever get the feeling that you're wasting your time, that you should really be someplace else doing something completely different?"

He examined her like she was a cartoon turning into a human being. He was surprised that she spoke so softly with a complicated blend of powerlessness and strength.

"I think everyone feels that way sometimes," he offered.

He didn't know whether he should go back to work on the organizing task that Nadine had given him. She didn't seem nearly finished, but he wasn't sure whether she was going to say more so he motioned toward the stack of books that he needed to put price stickers on and reached for the pricing gun.

Nadine came out from behind her desk. This was the most casually she'd been dressed in the whole time David had worked at the bookstore but in her pin-striped skirt and black knit turtleneck, she looked like a runway model to him. Against all David's expectations, she took a seat on the table where he was working, right next to the stack of books he was about to handle. She looked like a kid sitting on a kitchen counter, waiting to watch an adult make a tasty snack.

"I can't concentrate anyway," she said, as though reading his mind. "And who's kidding who? We're a dream team down here, light years faster than Hank even needs us to be, so let's just take a breather, shall we?"

"Sure," he said apprehensively. Until the words came out of her mouth, David never would have imagined that Nadine would ever 'take a breather'.

"I know," she said, "let's do something fun. I have an idea."

She got up off the table and went to her purse. Change purse in hand, she made a dash for the door. "I'll be back."

David shook his head at the absurdity of it all. He wondered where she was off to and figured that he'd better hurry up and price the books in front of him while he had the chance. Even if Nadine was pretending to be a slacker, he knew that there was nothing lazy about her and that she valued being miles ahead of Hank's expectations.

She came back only a couple of minutes later. Whatever she had with her must have been from the vending machines right outside the store.

"Here," she said, handing him a brightly colored wax paper package.

"A Popsicle?"

She nodded. He laughed. "So this is your idea of a fun time, eh?"

"Yeah," she nodded, tearing open her package. "I live on the edge. I know."

He opened his. "Oooh. Orange. My favorite."

"Really? Because I gave you the underdog," she said, smiling. "I wanted to keep the pink one for myself."

"I'd have given you pink if it were up to me." David held up his Popsicle to hers, as though it was a cocktail and he was about to say 'cheers'. Instead he said, "To Popsicle compatibility. It's a rare and beautiful thing."

Chapter Six

David crammed his book bag into his little locker in the staffroom and took his place at the cash register on the textbook floor of the university bookstore on the first day of classes in September. The line up snaked around the building with students holding spots for each other while they ran to the coffee shop for lattes and muffins to endure the interminable process of buying course material. David had been lucky to get this job as he was only in his second year. These union jobs were coveted and only a select few students got chosen to make such a sweet hourly wage. Today was the day he had trained for. This was it. The next four hours would be the longest of the entire semester and if he could make it through today, he'd be able to handle the rest of the three-week contract, no problem.

By ten-thirty, his brain was mush. There were so many numbers and codes to remember. Out of the corner of his eye, he saw a delicate hand reach through the crowd with a cup of steaming coffee that had his name on the outer cardboard sleeve. He looked up to see the stunning Nadine smiling at him.

"I thought you could use a pick-me-up," she said.

Never had he been so grateful. "Thanks." He wanted desperately to follow that one word with something witty or enthusiastic but he couldn't muster it. At noon, on his fifteen-minute break, he wanted to reciprocate but he couldn't make it to the coffee shop and back unless he skipped lunch, and he was famished.

In the staffroom, he got out his sandwich and crammed a corner into his mouth, feeling like a rabid dog. Once his blood sugar level was balanced and he had calmed down enough to not be dizzy from numbers and voids and answering all kinds of inane student questions, he realized that he should write her a note. But what could a lowly cashier say to the woman everyone at the bookstore thought of as the goddess.

He wrote— *You made my day. I am eternally thankful. David.* He folded it in four and drew a happy face on the front. Before giving himself time to rethink the manliness — or lack thereof — of the smiley face, he marched into her department, saw her at her desk talking on the phone, quietly walked over to where she was sitting and slipped her the note. She signaled for him to stay.

He only had another minute left but when a goddess asks you to stay, you stay. So he waited for her to get off the phone then told her, "I'm so sorry but my break is up and Hank will have my neck on the chopping block if I'm not up there on time."

"Well then, you'd better hustle," she said.

"Yeah," David said, feeling incredibly shy. He didn't know how to talk to women like Nadine, women whose flirtation and energy were effortless. Why had she singled him out with the coffee? The question permeated the back of his mind for the rest of the shift.

There was the obvious explanation, of course. He had helped her achieve her goal. In the time he had worked in the basement with her, he had done a good job. Could it be that there was more to it?

He was off at one in the afternoon and hurried to his first class, but as the professor waxed on, David found his mind returning again and again to Nadine Baxter. He didn't like to admit it—especially to himself—but the cup of coffee she'd given him was the most action he'd gotten in a long time. Guys who don't do well with girls in high school are supposed to thrive at university. That's what his brother had said. But this was not David's experience. If anything, high school proved superior because at least in high school he had a lot of friends who were girls from his year's book club and extra-curricular activities. Since arriving at UMich on a full scholarship, he'd found himself in his dorm room alone a lot, surfing personals ads of tons of supposedly horny women, although the online community didn't offer a lot of prospects. David concluded that he was just not compatible with most women.

He tried to let go of the image of Nadine Baxter, dressed in her sexy form-fitting cream cardigan and black skirt with her hair tied back in a chignon. She was the perfect naughty librarian. On the surface, everything about her was professional and confident, but there was also a softness about her, an unspeakably feminine trait that had every young buck at the bookstore in knots whenever they found themselves in her vicinity counting and pricing the textbooks—whether they admitted to it or not. She controlled that operation and everyone knew it. Technically, the manager was in charge, but he had long since perceived that Nadine knew exactly how to whip a crew into shape and that she was far more successful at getting the bookstore lads to clear and shelve entire skids of books in record time than Hank or anyone upstairs. It was really something to get to work for her. She was a bossy perfectionist and it was a pleasure to appease such a stern mistress. David was grateful that he'd swapped shifts with Chrissy for those glorious weeks before school had started.

* * * *

When his philosophy lecture was over, David headed straight for the coffee shop to buy a gift card to present to Nadine, as a way to keep the exchange of offerings alive. From there, he went to the bookstore, still buzzing with students on the textbook floor. He took the stairs down to Shipping, marched into her realm and went right up to her desk where she was filling out paperwork.

"Thanks again for this morning. Allow me to return the favor. If you're up for it, I'd love to join you sometime."

"Oooh," she said in a tone that both surprised and delighted him.

Her response made him wonder how long ago it had been that someone had asked her out.

"Thanks. Are you free after work?" Nadine asked.

"When are you off?"

She glanced at the clock. "In an hour."

"I'll wait for you at Higher Grounds and if you can make it, awesome."

"And if not?" Her smile threatened to make him dizzy but he stayed focused and nodded.

"Then I'll get my homework done."

He turned on his heel and walked out, silently berating himself for the school-boy comment. Maybe she was checking him out, but he didn't dare look back in case it was only his own false perception.

* * * *

In the coffee shop, he tried to do some work, but his mind couldn't focus. Instead, he tried to dissect what had just happened. If he played his cards right, there was a chance that this could be a date, he surmised.

He'd managed to get a bit of reading done and he'd gotten back to someone over a phone message before the goddess entered the student hangout, came over to where he was and sat down.

"Hi, David," she said. He got up, trying to be a gentleman.

Immediately he recognized the flaw in his plan. She was far too sophisticated for this place. Sure, she picked up coffee here when she was at work, but she didn't look like a university student or like the kind of woman who would spend time in a place like this.

"Nadine," he began. "I'm so glad you agreed to meet me. Let's get off campus, I want to take you somewhere better."

She laughed. "What's this about?"

"Sorry?"

"Well, you wanted to see me for something, right?"

He panicked. She had not considered this to be a date. It was obvious. He was a hopeful little boy, like a student who goes to the high-school dance and asks his teacher to be his partner.

"I just wanted to thank you for making my morning." He smiled. He had to win her over, make her see what he saw in terms of the possibilities between them.

"Oh, you didn't have to."

"It's not every day that a beautiful goddess does something nice for me." David didn't see any reason to play it cool. Nadine was out of his league. It didn't take much to figure that out. At least, he thought, he might get points for enthusiasm.

"Goddess?" She looked shocked.

He nodded.

"I hardly think so," Nadine said. "But thank you just the same. Flattery gets you everywhere," she joked.

Much to her own surprise, Nadine was really turning on the charm for this guy. She didn't know what it was about him. On the surface, maybe it was his sandy brown hair and broad chest, his crystal blue eyes and the intensity of his gaze. She could never date him, she reasoned, since he was probably almost a decade — or more — younger than she was. But there was no harm in looking. At least that's what she had thought until she found herself unable to avert her eyes.

What was the harm in staying? She had wondered whether David had asked her as a date or whether he really was planning on doing homework and just wanted her to stop by for some reason. She pulled out a chair.

"I don't have much time," she said, answering the question she'd left hanging earlier about going off campus.

"What'll you have?" David asked, springing up to get her order at the counter.

"Just a grapefruit juice or something like that," Nadine said.

As she watched him line up behind a group of people who were also way younger than she was, Nadine grew self-conscious. She worried that grapefruit juice would make her seem sour and that was the very reputation she disliked. She knew what the young folks said about her and she would have joined their ranks seven or eight years ago, but things were different now. They didn't understand that. After the idealistic phase of one's twenties, one had to get a plan, have goals, make a future. What the hell was she doing ignoring all her plans to hang out with this younger guy?

"Here you are." David put a small plastic bottle in front of her.

"Thanks," she said. She wanted to leave. This was a mistake. Instead, she untwisted the cap and took a sip, then smiled awkwardly at her tablemate.

"So, Nadine, what do you do in your free time?"

Nadine scoffed at the question. "What free time?" She shook her head, but realized it was rude of her. He knew nothing about her. She explained, "I'm spending every spare moment getting my ducks in a row. I'm trying to launch a business."

"Whoa. Really? But you work full-time."

"Yep. That's why I don't have time for much else."

"So you're...single?"

"Yes." The word was still foreign to Nadine. It made her think of her aunts and their scorn for what they called old maids. She was almost afraid to admit her status to David, for fear that it might spread throughout the bookstore as another reason to talk about her behind her back.

"That's cool," he said with a grin that gave away his intention. "Me too."

Nadine was incredulous. Was he trying to pick her up? It seemed so ridiculous, her being his boss and all. His long hair. Her professional attire. Absurd.

"What do you do in your spare time?" Nadine said, in an effort to change the topic.

"I don't have a lot, either. I'm reading a lot these days. School's got me pretty busy."

"What are you studying?"

"Philosophy."

Nadine wanted to roll her eyes. It figured that this hippie dreamer spent his days and nights contemplating the nature of reality. He was her polar opposite.

"And what are you going to do with that?"

"What do you mean?"

"Like…for a career?"

"I know metaphysics isn't exactly a career, but I'm committed to teaching myself how to think to the best of my ability. I believe that's the most noble thing anyone can aspire to."

"Did you say noble?" Nadine nearly laughed. "Who aspires for noble these days?"

"I do." David seemed earnest.

"But how are you going to make money?" *Seriously, is this guy planning on being a bum forever or what?*

"I don't care about that. Money is nice, but it isn't everything. When you have enough to cover your basic needs, I think it's natural to move on to loftier pursuits."

"Like swaying in a hammock?"

"Who said anything about that? You don't know much about philosophy, do you?"

Nadine shrugged. She knew enough to avoid filling her life with useless garbage.

"I studied practical stuff, I guess."

"Well, it doesn't get much more practical than philosophy. I mean, it can really change your life."

"How?"

"Years ago, I was depressed. Then I came across Marcus Aurelius. You know what he said? He said that very little is needed to make a happy life. It's all within yourself, in your way of thinking."

"Was he strumming on his guitar when he said that?" Nadine smirked. It was just too much for her, this idealistic conversation. She couldn't help but make fun of it.

"No, he was a Roman emperor." David was obviously annoyed. "He was a powerful tyrant."

"Sorry," she said. "I'm just a bit cynical."

"Oh?"

"It's been a shitty couple of years," she said. As soon as the words were out, something in her decompressed. It was the verbal equivalent of letting her hair down.

"It has if you *think* it has."

"It has," Nadine insisted.

"Not objectively. It hasn't been a shitty couple of years for me. And there are probably good things that happened in your life, too, but if you're looking for the shitty stuff, you'll find it. It's called false pattern recognition."

"Okay, Mr. Wisdom. If you say so. Then I suppose I just imagined the misery of my grandfather's death, my fiancé ditching me and getting laid off."

Nadine started to collect her things. It was time to go.

"I'm sorry," David said. "I never meant to imply that you imagined any of those things."

"Good. Because I didn't." She was defensive. *Who is this young know-it-all to tell me what my life is like?*

"I'm just trying to say that I figured out that it all starts up here." He pointed to his temple and tapped the side of his forehead a few times. "I used to think reality was objective, too. That bad things happen and they're just bad. But now I'm interested in how to think about reality, how to perceive it. It's the only thing that matters, really."

"This is a little over my head. I have work to do."

"I know you do, Nadine. I know you're serious and I like that about you. I'm the same way."

David could tell from the expression on her face that Nadine doubted that very much. After all, she had stuff to do and he was able to spend the rest of the afternoon waxing on about reality.

"Thanks for the grapefruit juice," she said.

With that, she was gone.

Chapter Seven

David floated home. Sure, their conversation hadn't been perfect. He knew she thought he was a flake, but he'd learned some valuable stuff. She was single. She was fierce and independent. She had a vision that she was working toward. She was unlike any other girl he knew.

David had grown tired of good time girls. There were plenty back on the beaches in Cuba. They were all over campus, too. Pre-lecture banter all around him told him that on weekends the girls in his classes got drunk and did things they later regretted. He didn't even want to hear the particulars.

In Nadine he saw a spark of something deeper. He was honored that she could be so vulnerable with him. She trusted him with intimate information. And when she looked at him, he sensed that she wasn't happy. There was something missing and he hoped that it was him.

His roommates had rented a movie and were about to start it when he opened the door.

"Wanna join us, man?" Chris asked.

"What are you watching?"

"*Weird Science.*"

"Seriously? Classic. I'm in."

Joining them in the living room, he cracked open a beer and sat back to relive one of his favorite movies from adolescence. His roommates, like him, could quote most of the scenes. By the time they got to the part where the boys augment the breasts of the cyber girl they invent, David was already on his second beer and the room had the same energy as the scene in the movie. Boys in the movie and boys in the shared apartment all said it, in perfect unison—"Bigger, bigger."

David thought about Nadine. How embarrassed he'd be if she knew that this was his idea of a good time. But when Kelly LeBrock appeared in front of the fictional boys, his heart skipped a beat, for this was the same feeling he'd had today. It was a combination of total arousal and deep, deep awareness of inadequacy. What can a couple of pasty little nerds offer a real woman? And so it was with Nadine. Even looking around the living room told him they could never be together. This place was furnished with a couch and chairs they'd found in the alley when they moved in. They had milk crate shelves, for God's sake! Kelly LeBrock would have laughed and walked out.

David was by no means a nerd, like the guys in *Weird Science*, but he felt like one when he thought of Nadine. In a couple of years, he planned to move into his own place, buy real furniture and have a real job. Then, maybe, he'd stand a chance with her. But as things stood right now, they seemed worlds apart. More than anything, he wanted to fast forward to a time when she might consider him. He went to his room. His closet was full of jeans and T-shirts, clothes that did not fit with Nadine's pencil skirt and blouse. He did have one nice shirt that his cousin had bought for him for a job interview years ago. He hadn't got the job, but the shirt was still there. Maybe if he ironed it and paired it with his best jeans, he could feign compatibility with Nadine. But he quickly realized that one good shirt could not take him far. He knew what he needed to do. The only problem was he hated shopping.

* * * *

It was Saturday night and Nadine had granted herself the evening off. It had been ages since she'd gone anywhere. Marnie and their other friend, Alfonso, had invited her out for martinis. She got there late and the drinks had clearly been flowing.

"Hey, girl!" Alfonso shouted as he waved at her from across the crowded lounge. She waved back. At the table, he stood up and kissed each of her cheeks. Marnie hugged her.

"See that guy over there?" Alfonso whispered as he gestured to a bartender who clearly worked out regularly. Nadine nodded. "Marnie and I are competing for him. Who do you think stands a better chance?"

"Come on," Marnie insisted. "He's totally been making eyes at me since we got here. I got this one. You already had that guy at Starbucks."

Alfonso rolled his eyes. "Bitch."

Nadine needed this. Watching her friends being goofy reminded her that there was plenty more to life than trying to make a go of a business. All those nights of crunching numbers and browsing commercial rental space had made her batty.

"I need a gin and tonic," she said.

She didn't want to wait for someone to come and take her order, so she put her coat down on the booth bench beside Marnie and turned toward the bar.

"You're going up there? Don't embarrass us," Alfonso said.

"Um, you're doing a pretty good job of that yourselves." She walked across the packed room filled with perfume and cologne-scented fashionable people. Nadine winked at her friends from the counter while she straightened her skirt. Her outfit was way too uptight, she thought, and so she unbuttoned the top part of her blouse. Still, it was very office-y.

The bartender with the invisible bull's-eye on him courtesy of her friends was actually pretty friendly. He smiled at her.

"What can I get you?"

"Double gin and tonic," Nadine answered, not giving in to the coyness of his stare, even though she, too, found him ridiculously cute. Some guys were just like that — cute in an untouchable way.

She got back to the table.

"So?" Her friends eyed her expectantly. "Gay? Straight? Attached? Single?"

"I don't know. It wasn't an interview."

They both shook their heads at her.

"Don't you two think about anything other than men?"

"Not really," Alfonso said.

"I do," Marnie said. "But it's never as fun as thinking about men."

Nadine took a sip of her drink. "To my friends. May you one day be guided by something other than your libidos."

"What the hell kind of toast is that?" Alfonso objected. "Look, I know you haven't gotten laid in way too long but don't be hating on us for looking."

Marnie nodded.

"Fine," Nadine relented, feeling like the big sister in the group. "To Saturday night."

"That's more like it," Alfonso said. "So where've you been anyway? You don't come out anymore."

"The bookstore. The business. It's all kind of taking a toll. I'm in bed by ten o'clock most nights."

"Is it me or does it sound like she's talking about a baby every time she mentions the new business?" Alfonso asked Marnie. He added a semi-disgusted look for effect.

"It totally does," Marnie nodded. "Sorry, Nadine. It's true, though."

"Okay, I know I've been kind of lame lately, but I'm stressed about making it. I'm putting everything on the line for this."

"Well, not really, since you're working full-time."

"I need the paycheck and the health insurance."

Marnie shook her head at Nadine then gave her a slightly mocking caress on the cheek. "You and security." She shook her head again.

Nadine was going to defend herself, but there was no point. Marnie had known her for so many years, and she was right.

"I'm accustomed to a certain lifestyle. Is that so weird?"

"It's not weird at all," Alfonso said. "It's just that you're working full-time and trying to work at your business full-time and, well, sooner or later, something's gonna give."

"Don't say that." Nadine dreaded the thought. She had nightmares about things going wrong.

"I'm just sayin'. When's the last time you cut loose? Had some fun? When was the last time you had sex?" he asked.

"Um." Nadine tried to do the math but it was a blur. "Can we just change the subject?"

They looked at each other. "Nope."

"There's even this sexy young guy at her work who's totally crushing on her," Marnie told Alfonso.

"Oooh," he said. "Do tell."

"It's nothing," Nadine protested and took another sip of her drink.

"Name?"

"David."

"Mmm. Sexy biblical name," Alfonso said. Nadine punched him in the arm.

"Nothing's gonna happen," Nadine insisted.

"Why not?"

"Because he's way too young."

"How young?"

"One of the students."

"Oh my God! That's illegal," Alfonso exclaimed.

"A university student," Nadine said, irritated. "Geez. Don't make it worse than it is."

"So how old is he?"

"I don't know for sure. Over twenty, I hope."

"Girl, you are wild," Alfonso kidded. "I take it all back."

"Nothing's happened. And, like I said, nothing will."

"Why not?" Alfonso said.

"Because I don't want to have to hear 'barely legal' jokes every time I hang out with my friends."

Nadine loathed teasing and had really never been good at taking a joke. Her friends could tell by her suddenly serious tone that she'd had enough.

Marnie's face changed from playful to her familiar best friend. "I think you should ask him out."

"Come on!" Nadine said. "Would you two just knock it off?"

"You obviously noticed him. He has the wicked hots for you, too. So why not?"

"Yeah, girl. Get yourself laid."

She wondered if she was really that uptight. She didn't even need to ask her friends for their opinion on the matter. She turned the tables on Alfonso.

"It's so easy for you guys. Twenty minutes and you're done."

"It is not always like that," he protested. "I will have you know that sometimes it only takes ten."

Marnie burst out laughing. "Guys are so lucky. Why do we have to get all mushy and overthink-y and manipulate-y?"

"I can't answer that," Alfonso said.

"Well, I envy you, too," Nadine said. "And you know, maybe it wouldn't be the worst thing. I mean he's stupid hot. And I've never used anyone for sex before."

"Don't think of it as using," Alfonso said. "He wants it, too."

But the scenario had become too real, too fast. Just thinking about the recent conversation with David made Nadine nervous. He'd gotten to her somehow. She kept mulling over his words, all that Roman emperor stuff. What was he talking about? She was hopeless. If she was already overthinking David's perspective now, what would happen if she actually slept with him? Nadine took another sip and decided to change the topic for good.

"Hey, Marnie, I think the bartender looked over here," Nadine said, hoping to distract her friend from further scrutiny.

"If he did, he was definitely checking me out," Alfonso declared. They looked at each other like they were going to arm wrestle over it. Nadine laughed. She was glad that she had come out. She had needed this.

* * * *

David called his friend Nick in the afternoon. "Dude, you gotta come shopping with me." He needed someone with good fashion sense and, as far as he knew, Nick dressed himself, unlike some of the other guys they worked with whose girlfriends were the real decision-makers.

"Why, man?" Nick sounded skeptical.

David wasn't going to beg, so he changed his tactic. "Come on, I'll buy you dinner at the food court."

"All right, fine."

They arrived at the mall. Nick was immediately distracted by a booth featuring plastic kitchen trinkets.

"Oh, man, I totally need one of these," he said, picking up a salad spinner.

"Dude. Concentrate."

"What the hell, man? Since when are you so hung up on clothes?"

"I just..." David didn't really have an explanation that seemed adequate. "I, uh..."

"This is about a chick, isn't it?"

"Um, well, yeah."

"Why didn't you say so, man?" He slapped David on the arm. "What's she like? Who is this secret vixen?"

"No one." David instantly regretted bringing it up. Could anyone understand his feelings for Nadine?

"Dude, you just said."

"Yeah, but I don't think she'd ever go for me."

"You can't think like that, man. That's for chumps. All right, here's what we're gonna do. We'll start at the food court. You can tell me all about her. Then we'll shop. Get you all set up." He affectionately slapped David's chest and made a little circle with his palm.

Over teriyaki beef, David told him everything without disclosing that he was talking about Nadine.

Nick listened intently. "Seems like you really dig this girl."

"I do," David confessed. "I think it might be more than a crush."

"Well, don't go getting ahead of yourself."

"I haven't felt like this before."

"Maybe not, but girls don't like it when guys come on too strong. Don't be moving in with her in your mind just yet. Give her some space. Get her used to the idea."

"All right, all right. So what kind of look should I go for?"

"Honestly, we need to do a whole makeover, man."

"What?"

"When's the last time you had your hair cut? I know someone talented."

"Just clothes today."

"All right, all right. Let's see. I'm thinking semi-professional. Young. Hip. Artsy. We'll work with what you got."

Once they'd discarded their trays, they headed for Banana Republic. David tried on pants that weren't jeans for the first time since his mom had made him wear Sunday clothes. The khakis looked good on him, the salesgirl said. So did the three collar-shirts and two sweaters, one of which was argyle. He even saw a leather messenger bag that looked a lot better than the backpack he'd been sporting.

David passed the sales girl his Visa.

"Hey, man, when'd you get a gold card?"

"I dunno. They just sent it to me."

"God. Must be nice," Nick said.

"I don't really use it much."

He signed the slip and they walked out. David felt like a new version of his older self had started to assert himself. He was looking forward to wearing his new clothes to work.

Chapter Eight

The textbook rush was over but the bookstore had extended David's contract. On the days when it wasn't busy upstairs at the cash registers, he was sent down to help out in Shipping and Receiving, a request he was rather sure came from Nadine.

"This is a different look for you," Nadine said, as soon as he came through the doors in the clothes Nick and the salesgirl had chosen for him.

He was vindicated. It was worth it to leave the plaid shirt in the laundry hamper back home. He merely shrugged in acknowledgment of her comment.

"Just a side to me you haven't seen yet," he said.

"Hmm," she said. "What's next? Are you going to cut your hair and shave your beard?"

"This?" David tugged at his wolverine pelt. "Never."

Nadine smiled as though she approved of his choice to keep the beard. He couldn't help but notice how truly uncharacteristic this conversation was for Nadine.

"So, I've got a skid for you," Nadine said, gesturing to the plastic-wrapped gigantic cube in the middle of the room.

"Cool. I've missed this."

"You have not," she said.

"You don't know that. I have. I dream of clearing skids for you," he said, wondering if he was laying it on too thick. She laughed, so it was probably okay.

"Well, then..."

"Uh-huh. Gimme the price gun and the paperwork and I'll get 'er done."

"Dependable. I like that."

She was torturing him. It was awful and delicious and horrible and fantastic, all at once. He wanted to sweep her into a wild and passionate embrace and kiss her like they were in the movies, but they were not. He had a job to do. She had expectations. She went and sat at her desk and did not, as far as he could tell, look at him again.

* * * *

After a few hours, David was sweating from hauling books off the skid onto the cart. He stopped working and took his sweater off. Underneath he wore a T-shirt that showed off his built frame. He was surprisingly muscular. He tossed the sweater on the utility table next to him.

"Did you go shopping recently or what?" Nadine asked, looking up for the first time in ages.

"Yeah, actually."

"Well, good choice. The sweater, I mean. But don't dress up for this place," she said.

"You do."

"Yeah, but I'm not lifting all those books off the skids."

"You make a point." He didn't want to tell her that he'd expressly changed his appearance for her. That would never do. Instead, he kept on working in silence.

Nadine finally interrupted. "I miss shopping."

"Why? I hate shopping."

"You do? No! You did such a good job of it. Don't tell me you hate it. It's shopping. Everything about it is great."

"Not to me. I'd sooner live in a communist country where there are more important things to worry about than the latest fashion."

"You don't mean that," Nadine said, getting up. She sat on the table next to him, dangling those perfect legs of hers in front of him. She was ruthless.

"I do indeed," he insisted.

"Wow. A genuine hippie," she said in a teasing voice.

"Busted." He shrugged. "Material possessions are overrated — that's all I'm saying."

"You wouldn't say that if you were homeless."

"No, I wouldn't. But above a certain socio-economic level — and not even a very high one, like I'm talking roof over your head sort of thing — you don't really need much."

"Oh, to be young again."

He looked at her. She was smiling, having her fun with him.

"Let me ask you something," David said.

"Sure."

"Why do you work so hard?"

She looked taken aback. "Why wouldn't I?"

"Well, why would you?"

"Um, I have to. Stability. Health insurance. Home. Car. Clothes."

"See, that's the foundation of consumer society — all that crap."

"Oh, and are you going to try to undo centuries of Western capitalism with your philosophy now?"

"Not at all. But I would like to point out that we all have a choice. I try not to overcomplicate my life with too many belongings. I've never wanted to own a lot of stuff."

"Yeah, but that's what it's like to be your age."

"Any age."

"You'll probably change your mind. You'll see."

"Don't condescend."

She put her hands up like she was caught in the act of doing something illegal. Her lips curled downward.

"You know, one thing I'm really curious about is why anyone would sell themselves short in this life and put work before their dreams."

Nadine's shoulders tensed. "Because not everyone is comfortable with poverty. Some of us have aspirations."

She got up off the table and walked back to her desk.

David knew he had to keep the conversation going or it would forever be over.

"I'm just saying that it's not worth it to stress out too much about stuff. That's all. I mean, it's good to be able to walk into a store and buy a sweater because you like it, but it's not the best part about being alive."

Nadine scrunched her face up. "Do tell. What's the meaning of life?"

"Well, I'm not sure. I mean, if *Macbeth* is right, it's a tale told by an idiot and it signifies nothing. I don't believe that, though. I really don't know. All I know is that it isn't about shopping."

"Not for you."

"You're right. It's relative. It's different for everyone."

Nadine rolled her eyes. "Why do I bother? All I meant to tell you is that I kind of miss the days when I was carefree and able to buy whatever I wanted because my life made sense."

"Doesn't your life make sense now?"

She shook her head. "Not really. Most days I feel like I'm herding cats. Starting a business is a heck of a lot of work and I... I don't know, I sometimes wonder why I bother."

"Because you have a vision. You're building something."

"I guess. I kind of wish I could just go for a manicure, though."

"So, why don't you?"

"Because I'll ruin it in two seconds. I work with my hands."

"You have beautiful hands as is. You don't need a manicure."

"That's nice of you to say," Nadine said, examining her nails. "But you're dead wrong. I have man hands."

"You most definitely do *not* have manly looking hands. You are the epitome of femininity," David said, self-conscious suddenly that he had overstepped. He approached her desk and took her hands in his, as though he'd been invited to inspect for himself.

Nadine's palms were soft, her fingers long and lean.

* * * *

That night, Nadine went home to her beautiful town house, haunted by David's observations about materialism. Did she need to live in the same big home she had once shared with Allan? She could downsize and save more money that way. But it would be a step down and she'd had so many of those in the past couple of years.

She called Marnie.

"How's the boy toy?" Her best friend sure knew how to cut to the chase.

"I don't want to talk about it."

"You like him."

"I can't help it. I don't have time for a real relationship. This is the best I've got."

"Hell, it's better than me. Don't knock it."

"I'm not," Nadine said, pouring herself a glass of water. "I don't know what to do, though. I mean, he's a student. He works for me."

"Meh," Marnie said.

"What does that mean?"

"It means *meh*. So what? Who cares? Have some fun. It's not going to kill you."

"But…"

"What? You could lose your job? It's a shit job, Nadine. You don't want it anyway."

"Damn it, you're right."

"And don't go telling me that whole principled bullshit about age. Allan was age appropriate and perfect on paper, but the guy was a dick."

"I know."

"Don't date another dick," Marnie admonished.

"David's not a dick."

"That's why I'm saying go for it. I saw the way he looked at you. I don't think you get a lot of chances in life with non-dicks who look at you like that. Know what I'm saying?"

"But…"

"Don't be sensible, Nadine. For once in your life, don't be sensible. I mean, I love you and all but I can't stand by and watch you go through another Allan scenario. Let's never repeat that. But I also can't sit idly by and watch you deny yourself something that could be great just because you—like me—need to have everything seem perfect on paper. Life is not paper."

Nadine thought of David. She thought he would enjoy that line. He would agree with it. But as far as showing him how she felt went, she was lost.

Chapter Nine

Nadine noticed that David did everything to satisfy her demands and worked as though his life depended on it. Was there more to it than job performance and work ethic? If she wanted a skid cleared in four hours, he did it in three. If she wanted the warehouse tidied, he color coded boxes and invented new systems.

One Thursday afternoon Nadine snuck up on him collapsing boxes for recycling. When she spoke, he seemed shocked, as though he had not noticed she'd been standing behind him.

"What are you doing this weekend?" she asked. She tried to sound casual and objective, as though he could easily have plans that did not involve her.

"Me? Um. Not much. You?" He could not disguise his nervousness.

"I just got Apple TV. I might watch a movie," she said.

He nodded. "That sounds lovely."

"Yeah."

"Alone?" David asked.

"Maybe. Unless. Well, would you like to come over?" Nadine was shocked at herself. She wished she could have recorded the moment for Marnie. No way would her best friend believe that she had actually asked him over.

"Yes," David exclaimed. "I mean, sure. Yeah. That sounds good."

"Great."

"Great."

* * * *

David was tremulous walking up the front steps of the heritage house. It was the first time he'd gone to the home of a woman who didn't live with her parents or in a dorm. When he knocked on the door, he felt sweaty.

"Come in," she said, holding a glass of white wine. "Let me take your jacket."

"Thanks," he said. Then, looking around, he added, "Nice place."

"I'll get you some wine and show you around." Nadine paused and added, "Or water or soda or something."

"I'll take wine," he said, his palms desperately wet. He followed her into the kitchen where she poured him a glass. He'd never tried white wine before.

"The house is sort of neat," Nadine explained. "It's got three suites, but it isn't divided by floors, like most shared houses. I've got three little floors. Here's my kitchen and living room and upstairs is the bedroom."

David thought he blushed when he thought of her bed. "What's downstairs?" he asked.

"Oh, my business."

This was definitely the opening David had been waiting for. "What is it that you do outside of the bookstore?"

"I restore antique furniture."

David pictured the sexy goddess using a sanding block. He couldn't imagine her actually doing physically intensive work like that, so his vision was rather porn inspired. He saw her in overalls with nothing underneath. He smiled at his own imagination.

"Oh." All of the blood cells in David's body rushed to his cock and he felt himself stiffen beneath the constraints of his jeans, so he casually turned toward the counter and hid his pelvic area from Nadine's view. What was it about the idea of her working with wood that turned him on so much? When he was quite young he'd seen a *Playboy* at a friend's house and the girl in the picture had been wearing nothing but a tool belt. He hadn't been able to think of women and tools together since without recalling that sight.

"Is that weird? Should I not have told you?" Nadine asked, suddenly coming across as much more vulnerable than at work.

"I'm glad you told me. Believe me. I'm just, uh, surprised, I guess. I pictured you as more of a girly girl. Don't get me wrong. It's really cool that you work with wood."

David wanted to kick himself for how that had come out. He added, "I just mean it figures that this is what your business would be."

"What do you mean it figures? You just said you never would have guessed."

"All I said was I was surprised. That's all."

Nadine beckoned him to follow her into the living room. When she flopped down on the couch in front of him in a perfectly effortless way, David sat on the ottoman next to the couch. His posture was stiff.

"Can I be frank?" he asked.

"Sure."

"You've got this energy about you. It's kind of...well...it's kind of all-consuming."

"Oh, please." She brushed off his compliment with an elegant flick of the wrist. But as he sat across from her, she enquired further, "What do you mean?"

"I mean that ever since you put that coffee in front of me, I've been trying to figure out why."

Nadine laughed as she leaned on the back edge of the couch. She relished his attention, craved it like a perfect dessert to end a fine evening.

"It's true," David said. "I can't pay attention in my classes. I might as well drop out."

"And do what?"

"Worship at your feet."

She laughed again. David was mesmerized by Nadine's incredible laugh—sincere and from the belly. It was nothing like the insecure giggles of girls his age. He saw in her something else entirely. She was a goddess in the real sense of it. She was an untouchable. It was taboo for mere boys to try to seduce real women. Everyone knew that. Sure, now and then you had your Ashton Kutcher and Demi Moore scenarios but such couplings invited scorn and criticism or outright mockery and always ended. Either way, it was not understood—not like David understood it—sitting there, across from Nadine, completely transfixed by her.

"You think I'm joking, don't you?"

"Yes, a little," Nadine said.

She was being perfectly honest. She really couldn't imagine how smitten David was with her because she had forgotten what puppy dog love was like. But in this moment, she felt alive again. She felt a flourish in her belly. He moved in closer to her, so close that she felt his knee brush against hers. She felt his desire to kiss her. She could see it in his faraway gaze and she wanted so badly to give in and let her mouth do what it wanted, but she couldn't let go of that part of her that nagged her with reason. *He's too young. You work together. It could never go anywhere.*

She sat up and her body was firm, maybe even rigid. It clearly jolted David back into alert awareness and immediate awkwardness. He took a step back. *I've ruined it.* She had sabotaged the best thing that had happened to her in a long time.

"David," she said, trying to ease the moment. "Sorry," she whispered.

He looked down. "I'm the one who should be sorry. I think I jumped to some kind of wrong conclusion."

"You didn't," she said abruptly. "David, I like you. I'm just aware of some key facts that, uh, well, keep this from being able to be a thing." She waved her right hand back and forth in the air, gesturing at the two of them. She shook her head.

"Why did you invite me here tonight?" David said in a tone that was hard to decipher.

"David," she began.

"Stop saying my name," he interrupted. "I know what it means when women do that."

"What?"

"That you're going to tear my heart out and eat it."

"Um, did you just accuse me of cannibalism?" She gave him a look of sarcastic chagrin.

He looked mortified as though he had suddenly realized what he'd said. He laughed. "That's not what I meant," he explained. He got up and moved to the couch.

"It's okay. I'm sorry if I sent mixed messages. I don't think anything can happen here because... Well, I'm considerably older than you."

"Really? I hadn't noticed." He said it playfully, teasingly. She couldn't help but smile too when she saw him beaming at her.

"And we work together," she argued.

"Not really. I'm on contract and, in fact, yesterday was my last shift."

"But you'll be back at the beginning of next semester."

"Not if you don't want me to," David said.

"But it's the best job on campus. You'd be an idiot not to come back. And you got a great performance review, so you know they'll ask you back."

"Maybe so, but if you didn't want me to come back, I would not come back. That's what I'm saying."

"Really?"

"Nadine, I'd do pretty much anything for you."

"What?" She cocked her head to one side and stared at him. "Nobody's ever said anything like that to me before."

"There is no way that's true. You are a liar, Nadine Baxter." His tone was sardonic, his face stern with mockery at her self-deprecation.

"I'm not. I'm being perfectly serious," she insisted.

She giggled in spite of her words. She couldn't help herself. The moment was suddenly hilarious to her. She felt so young all of a sudden.

"Well, I would do anything for a chance to get to know you a little better, even if it meant having to work twice as many hours somewhere else."

Her heart throbbed inside her chest. The sincerity in his eyes told her everything she needed in that moment. She needed nothing else but that feeling of certainty that this was right. She leaned in and kissed him. The second her lips touched his, he threw his arms around her and pulled her in close.

They settled into an embrace on the couch in Nadine's living room, where it was plush and warm, a little nest in the cold of autumn.

"What movie would you like to watch?"

"You choose," David said.

"I've been working my way through Hitchcock lately. I don't know if that's something you're interested in."

"I love Hitchcock. When I was in twelfth grade, I spent a whole paycheck on a pass to the Hitchcock film festival."

He regretted referencing high school immediately. He did not want to add that that had been just a few years ago.

"Have you seen *Spellbound*?"

"Yes, but I'll watch it again."

"Well, if you've seen it we can watch something else."

"No, *Spellbound* is perfect."

"Oh?"

"Yeah. You haven't seen it?"

"No."

"We have to see that one, then."

David was relieved.

"More wine?" she asked.

"Please," he said.

She went to the kitchen for refills. When she came back, she said, "You look comfortable." He had both arms spread out, one on the armrest, the other — suggestively — at the top of the couch, beckoning for her to sit down beside him and let him cradle her.

Nadine could not wait to feel David's arm around her. Watching the movie was just a formality. She'd have been happy to skip it. She sat down next to him and slowly, without seeming too eager, eased herself into the warm and safe comfort of his embrace. She could barely concentrate on the film but she was in heaven.

* * * *

By the time the movie was over, Nadine had fully curled up into David's embrace. There was no mistaking it. They were cuddling. He had been so hyper aware of her beside him all throughout the movie. He was glad that he'd already seen the movie before because otherwise he would have had no idea what it was about. The smell of her hair was intoxicating and when he looked down, he could see her cleavage. He wondered if she was aware of how she'd positioned herself. Did she want him to see it? Did she want to torture him?

Nadine turned off the television and sat up, leaning against the other armrest, though their bodies were still touching.

"I'm so glad I asked you to come over tonight," she said.

"Me too," he said.

"Maybe we can do it again sometime."

Sometime. It was the kiss of death, David thought. It really meant *never.* He didn't want to settle for that. He needed something more.

"How about tomorrow?" His eagerness betrayed him. He knew it wasn't good to play with open cards when dealing with a woman like Nadine. He pictured Nick giving him hell for it.

"I wish I could. I have a deadline, actually," Nadine said.

"What kind of deadline?"

"A client brought a dresser and wardrobe to me and I told her I'd have them back to her by Tuesday, and they still need another coat of varnish then a beeswax treatment, so I've got a lot to do tomorrow and Sunday."

"Can I help?"

"No, no." She seemed utterly shocked at his offer, and he wondered if that was because she wasn't nearly as used to receiving help as he had assumed. Her oblique references to her ex had him curious as to whether he was the kind of guy who'd given her a hand when she needed it or if he was more self-centered. He couldn't imagine taking someone like Nadine for granted, but he had noticed that often the best kinds of girl were treated the most poorly.

"Well, can I come watch?"

She looked at him quizzically.

"I'll be good. I promise. I can bring my guitar and entertain you," he said, because if playing the hippie philosopher was a way to insinuate himself into her presence, he was happy to do it.

"Serenade me while I varnish in my coveralls? Hmmm. Well, that would be a first."

David could tell that Nadine didn't know how to answer. She pulled away and sat up in a stiff manner.

"Look, I'm on a mission, kick-starting a new life for myself, and if I'm going to turn my dream into reality, I can't afford to get distracted."

David understood her intention completely. He'd also had similar spurts of ambition and he knew that it took total concentration to achieve the stuff worth striving for.

"I respect that," he said. "I wouldn't get in your way. I'd just hang out and play music for you."

"David, I'm flattered by all this...attention, but I..."

"Okay," he interrupted. He didn't want to let her finish the sentence that could very well exclude him forever. "Well, what about next Friday? I have a Criterion collection edition of *Vertigo*. I could bring it over — or you could come to my place."

David pictured himself bribing his roommates. They'd clear out if he let them take his car and if he gave them twenty bucks each to go to the all you can eat Japanese buffet downtown. Then all he'd have to do was clean the place from top to bottom. No sweat.

"Yeah, why don't you bring it over next weekend?" she said. He breathed a sigh of relief. The longer he could delay her seeing his place, the better for him.

He took this conversation as his cue to leave. It would serve him best in the long run to be gentlemanly and considerate. She'd just agreed to see him again. This was it. They were dating.

"Nadine," he said, taking her hand in his. "Thanks for having me over." He got up. She followed him as he went to the door. He started to put on his shoes and jacket. He was thinking about how he might be able to steal a kiss.

Nadine opened the door for him. He was about to go without a kiss when all of a sudden, he knew he'd kick himself if he didn't make it happen.

"Nadine?" he asked.

"Yes?"

"I had a really nice time tonight."

"I'm glad," she said. "Me too."

She motioned to hug him, and he opened his arms to her and without any hesitation, he kissed her. As soon as their lips touched, he closed his arms around her and held her tightly, his lips firm against hers. Kissing her felt so right. Nadine felt almost limp in his arms, as though she wanted him to hold her, take her, keep kissing her. Her eyes were closed and her arms were around him.

After a couple of minutes of unbridled passion had elapsed, they both simultaneously pulled back. David noticed that Nadine looked dizzy.

"Wow," she said. "I was not expecting that."

He took her hand again and this time he pulled it to his lips and kissed the back of it. He hadn't felt that kind of uncomplicated connection in ages.

"See you next Friday," she said.

"Yes, Friday." He took a step into the cold. "Goodnight, Nadine."

"Goodnight, David."

Chapter Ten

Nadine went back to her living room and flopped down on the loveseat. She hadn't experienced anything like that kiss in years, especially the way he'd taken her hand and kissed the back of it. She could still detect David's scent, a combination of detergent and a manly hint of musk. She was smitten. There was no denying it. Against her own rationale, she was deeply attracted to this young guy who gave her the delicious attention she'd been craving for so long. He didn't ask her about the future, about kids and weddings. He didn't seem to evaluate her against the rubric she'd grown accustomed to. That in itself was intoxicating. There was more to it, though. She got the sense that he had a pure heart, that he had a positive outlook on the world and that, too, was something she hadn't come across during the past decade. Perhaps the reason the corporate world was so exhausting and draining was that it required a certain cynicism and selfishness. She was so glad to be free of that and grateful for this evening of bliss.

Marnie called.

"How was your date with the boy toy?" she wanted to know.

"Um…well," Nadine didn't know how to put her feelings into words that her friend would understand.

"Oh no," Marnie said. "Don't fall for him, okay? He's just a baby. There's no way you two are actually compatible."

"You're the one who encouraged me!"

"Yeah. That should be your first clue. I don't know shit about men."

"He's not a baby, by the way. He knows himself better than a lot of people I know."

"Oh, please. He thinks with his penis, like every other guy."

Nadine changed the subject. She didn't want to spoil her precious evening by trying to convince her best friend of anything. She realized in that moment that it really didn't matter to her what anyone else thought. They discussed Marnie's co-workers instead.

* * * *

Nadine's brow was sweaty. The doors were wide open and the cool October wind permeated her workspace. The scent of varnish was strangely appealing, a reminder of her grandfather. How she missed him. It didn't take a degree in psychology to guess that Nadine's love of furniture restoration connected her to her childhood, which she had spent helping her granddad at Winston's Fine Furniture. She'd been so sad to see the business sell after his death but her parents didn't want it and she had been too busy with her supposed career. Selling the shop had been easy. Grandpa Winston had an excellent reputation and the turnkey operation was off the market two days after it was listed.

Her phone rang.

"It's David. Just wondering if you'd like some takeout. I know you're busy. I won't distract you. I just happened to be in your area and thought maybe it'd be hard to do everything you need to do and make food too."

"You're too sweet," she said. "I do have to eat."

"Great. I'll swing by with some Thai food in about half an hour."

How did he know that Thai food was her absolute favorite? She was almost finished with the final coat of varnish on the dresser but wouldn't have time to clean up and look presentable. She considered stopping but decided it was best if David saw the real her. Maybe it would change his puppy-dog infatuation and solve the problem of their relationship before it even began, she rationalized.

As she hurried through the last strokes, she couldn't help but wonder whether any of the guys she'd ever gone out with, especially Allan, would have come by with food for her, if she'd asked. Certainly none had ever called and offered.

* * * *

David, dressed in his best work clothes, pulled into Nadine's driveway at quarter to three in the afternoon. He had felt on top of the world driving home the night before and he knew that he had no reason to play it cool with Nadine. He had no interest in playing games with her and he figured she would either appreciate that about him or not, and it didn't much matter. He had to do what was right in his heart and that meant seeing as much of Nadine as possible.

He saw Nadine put down her brush and walk toward him, smiling in spite of the chilly gray afternoon. She threw her arms around him.

"Thanks for bringing lunch," she said.

"My pleasure."

"You really didn't have to."

"That's what makes it pleasurable." He gave her a telling smile.

He grabbed the bag of coconut curry and spring rolls and closed the door to his car. They walked up to her open garage.

"So let's see what you've got going on," he said. "Wow. Nice pieces." He examined the wardrobe and the dresser carefully.

"I'll show you the 'before' photo inside."

"Impressive finishing."

"Thanks. I'm not finished yet, though."

"Should we eat out here?"

"No, no," Nadine said. "Let's go upstairs and get out of the fumes."

He followed her up the stairs, through the living room they'd cuddled in mere hours earlier, into the kitchen where she gestured for him to put the bag of takeout on the table in the dining nook. He could imagine belonging here, being a regular part of her life. He felt comfortable in her surroundings and though he tried not to appear too comfortable too soon, he also wanted her to see him there.

"Where do you keep the plates?" he asked. "I'll get us set up while you go wash up from your work."

"Really?"

"Sure."

Nadine gave a brief overview of her kitchen then went to the bathroom to wash up. At the sink, as she exfoliated her hands, she recognized that something she'd only ever fantasized about was actually happening. A man had showed up to be supportive of her. This was highly unusual. He was making himself useful in the kitchen, and he was genuinely interested in her work. She looked at herself in the bathroom mirror. There wasn't a trace of makeup or pretense about her in this moment, yet here he was.

They ate lunch quickly.

"How did you come upon the pieces downstairs?" David asked.

"I'm still working on the ones for the woman who wants them on Tuesday. They're acquisitions from an old farm. Both are late nineteenth century, my favorite time period."

Once they had finished eating, David said, "Well, I'll take care of the dishes if you want to get back to work."

Nadine looked puzzled, as though she'd seen a unicorn. David paid her look no mind and took the plates to the sink. He packed the remainder of the food into containers and put them in her fridge. Then he got to work on the dishes.

Nadine went downstairs and was just about to start up again when David reappeared.

"So, what can I do to help?" he asked.

"What?"

"Let me help."

"You really don't have to. I'm fine."

"Four hands are better than two, and I'm kind of hoping you'll finish before the deadline so we can spend a bit of time together."

"Oh, I see," she said flirtatiously. "So this is a ploy to spend time with me?"

"Well, yeah. But I also really would love to help. I've been studying a lot lately and it's good for me to get my hands dirty now and then."

"All right, mister. I accept."

"Good. Show me what you'd like me to do and I'll try my best to impress you, just like in the bookstore dungeon."

"Let's not talk about that place right now," she said, but then she added, "You did impress me, by the way."

He smiled. "I tried."

She showed him what to do, how to apply the varnish, and let him take over on the wardrobe's back side to get the hang of it.

They set to work quietly and Nadine became aware that it might be awkward that she didn't have any music set up or anything. She liked to just be in her own thoughts when she worked. Maybe that was part of the appeal of furniture restoration—hours and hours of alone time. So she figured this was a good chance to get to know him.

"So, David," she began. "What do you want to be when you grow up?"

"Happy," he said immediately.

"No, I mean as a career."

"Whatever makes me happy," he reiterated.

She rolled her eyes. *Cocky, youthful answer.*

As though he could read her quizzical mind, David elaborated, "The way I see it, my life is an open book and I've only written a few pages. I took a couple of years off after high school to travel around and see something of the world and work on a couple of projects. I think I can be happy doing many things and being in many places."

"So no plans?"

"Well, I'm studying right now. I've been looking forward to it and I'm enjoying it, so I'll make the best of it and see what happens next."

Nadine was envious of the implicit freedom in David's answers. She had always meant to backpack through Europe, had always fantasized about drifting through life, but she'd never been gutsy enough to let go of her plans. Plus, she liked living in a nice home and having nice things. That's why she had got her degree in business administration. Like every other aspect of her life, it made sense.

"So a Bachelor of Arts?" she asked. "What are you going to do with that?" She could practically hear the judgment in her own voice. She sounded like her parents. She sounded like every guy she'd dated in the past decade. "I mean, after university?"

She wanted to let it go, change the topic, but somehow she was programmed to need these answers. She couldn't stop herself. It was as though she needed to be able to see him some years in the future, to see whether they were compatible.

"I'll deal with that when I get there."

"I see," she said, even though she didn't see at all. All she saw in his answer was student loans.

"I like to live in the now as much as possible," he said. "After all, this moment is the only one that matters."

She smiled. *I've got a crush on a hippie. This must be some kind of mix-up.* He was definitely not her type. She hadn't slept much all week because she'd been up late worried about her future. She'd been doing spreadsheets in her mind, calculating her business expenses — what it would take to get a commercial space to work from, whether she could ever make enough to support herself, when she could quit the bookstore. She was a planner through and through.

David's idealism was not amusing to her and there she had it—the catch. Sure, he was nice to her, made her feel desirable, brought her food, helped her out, but where could this really go, she wondered. They were so different.

"I get it," she said. "You don't want to commit to anything. That makes sense. You're young."

"It's not about commitment," he retaliated. "But nothing changes the fact that life is made up of moments, and all we ever have is the present moment. None of us can predict the future."

"No, but we can make plans."

"I guess. But think about all those planners whose lives were ruined by hurricanes and typhoons." He looked around. "Not to mention illness and death."

Nadine's heart fell. What had she expected from someone so young? She felt like a romantic fool for having any feelings for him at all. There was no way she could join him on Hippie Island. No way they could be beach bums together. For a week or two, maybe, but what was she thinking?

Nadine was in her head completely. The two sides of her nature dueled within her. On one side there was her free spirit, the part of her that questioned the impulse to get married and start a family with a socially acceptable mate. On the other side, there was the Nadine who played it safe, who believed in self-reliance and hard work and good investments. That was the Nadine she'd been with Allan. She wanted to change that part of herself, but she didn't know if she could ever get that safety oriented part of herself to chill out. She had never felt so confused.

David put down his brush and walked over to her. He put his arms around her and held her. She clung to him.

"I'm here. Right now. And this moment with you is all that matters," he said.

"Really?" she asked. It seemed like a line.

"Yes. And I don't have anything against people who make plans. I just don't want to fall prey to the fallacious idea that we can predict what the future will hold."

"I don't either," she said. "But that said, I'm still saving for retirement."

"Me too, but I refuse to live my life for RRSPs."

Nadine eyed him. "Benefits and savings plans are the main reason I returned to the bookstore."

"But you want to leave it to run your own business. That's pretty 'in the moment' of you."

Nadine smiled. David was a lot more perceptive than she gave him credit for.

"Let's finish up so I can take you upstairs," David said.

Nadine nodded. Her confusion was over. It was true that she didn't know what the future would hold. But she knew that right now she had a gorgeous man who was helping her and she would never regret spending the afternoon with him. She could never regret letting him dote on her and help her out with her new endeavor. It was terribly sweet of him and maybe this was her good karma to have this brief tryst with this sweet, puppy dog guy. She didn't know what it all meant and it didn't matter. One more coat of lacquer and they could call it a day.

Nadine wanted to ask David more about his travels, but she was afraid. It was a trigger — a reminder of all the unsatisfying years she'd spent behind a desk doing less than what she loved, being less than fully alive. She didn't have an opportunity to ask because David had questions of his own.

"So, what's it like to be back at the bookstore?"

She rolled her eyes. "You really want to talk about that place, don't you?"

He shrugged. "We did meet there."

"It's okay, I guess. It gets me a little depressed sometimes because of all the old, familiar faces."

"Oh yeah?"

"Yeah. I mean Sue Ellen, Hank, Amarjit, Toby and the whole trade books floor were all there when I started ten years ago."

"So?"

"So, have you ever heard them complain about their lives? Sometimes at staff meetings, I just want to wear earplugs because their conversations are exactly the same. Nothing has changed."

"Some people don't like change."

"I know, but most of these people complain about stuff they could totally fix if they wanted to—like Hank and how he wants to make a short film. He's still talking about that. Like, just make the damn film, you know?"

He nodded respectfully. He listened.

"What?" Nadine asked.

"Nothing."

"Seriously. What were you just thinking?"

"Well, just that it's not really your business what they do or don't do with their lives, so I don't know why it's getting you down."

"I'm just afraid of being like that, being one of them."

"Nadine, you are nothing like them."

"You say that so confidently, but sometimes I'm not convinced."

She had stopped applying lacquer. She stood up and took a step back to look at her accomplishment. The wardrobe was complete. It just needed to dry.

"I don't believe you," he said. David saw an artist standing before her glorious work. He saw her reverence for wood, for historical pieces, for understanding exactly what needed to be highlighted from the past, modernized and protected.

"No?" Nadine said in a low and humble tone.

"No. You left your other career to follow your heart. I don't believe for a second that you'd do that unless you believed deep inside that you'd be successful at it."

Nadine looked at him. He was still squatting on the floor, still brushing an awkward area in the underbelly of the dresser that nobody would ever see but it seemed to matter to him—just as it did to her—that it was covered.

"That's a really nice thing to say, David."

"Well, I'm a nice guy." He smiled and winked at her.

"I know."

"But I'm not just nice. Don't think I'm one of those pushover guys who's just interested in your friendship."

Nadine picked up on the animalistic suggestion in his words. She shared his instincts. She felt her own body's magnetic pull toward him, a call she had spent several weeks trying to ignore and the past twenty-four hours trying to stomp out like an out of control fire.

David stood up. The moment called for something more than words and he knew it. This was his chance to show her exactly what he meant, and he intended to. He took her by the hand and she curled into him, accepting his embrace. He could tell that she liked being in his arms, even if she was afraid. She had different ideas in her head. He could respect that. David could tell that Nadine was caught off guard by their connection, as he had been, and he understood that it was a different thing for her to contend with their age difference than it was for him. Not only did he not care, he was excited. It was refreshing and new and he understood that she had things to offer him that no girl his age ever could. Nadine had life experience, wisdom and the quiet confidence that only comes from years.

He looked down at her and she looked up. He took the back of her head in his hands and held onto her as he slowly edged his lips toward hers.

Chapter Eleven

Nadine was melting inside. She could feel his touch everywhere and she wanted to fall into his arms and let him hold her completely. She wanted to lose herself in kissing him. Her body wanted desperately to give in to the feelings she had for him but still her mind clung to some noisy inner voice that told her there was something wrong.

"David," she said, interrupting the moment, "I haven't really made up my mind about what to do about us."

"What's there to do?"

"I mean whether we should take this further."

When David looked in her eyes, he saw only her passion. It was the line on her forehead that revealed her reluctance. He let go of her and took a polite step back. "Well, do you want to?"

"Yes, I want to. I just don't know if it's a good idea."

"Doing what you want is always a good idea."

"I disagree," she said.

David felt the fire in her. He knew she was torn and although he didn't want her to do anything against her wishes, he also perceived that she wasn't seeing the situation accurately and that if she only could, she'd see just how great they could be together.

"All right," he said, and by the look on her face he knew he'd shocked her. Instinctively, she felt what his body wanted. She responded by wrapping her legs around him. He supported her with his strong arms. "We're going to do this your way."

"My way?" She giggled.

"I'm taking you upstairs where we're going to sit down and write a civilized pro-con list. That's how you roll, isn't it?"

"Actually" — she nearly snorted she was laughing so hard now — "I *am* pretty fond of them."

"It figures," he said, as he walked in through the garage door, turned the corner then walked her up two flights of stairs until they were in her living room. The whole time he held her in his arms she laughed. He knew that whether she was ready to admit it or not, she loved every second of being with him.

Upstairs, he put her down on the edge of her sofa. He took a notebook from her bookshelf and picked up a pen from the coffee table and handed them to her.

"First con," David said as though they'd agreed that she'd take dictation. "Age difference."

She nodded and wrote it down.

"Pros," he said. "Instant connection, incredible physical chemistry, mutual respect."

She smiled as she tried to write with the same speed with which he rambled off justifications for their possible union.

"Different life experiences," she said.

"Good one," he said, taking the notebook from her to write the words down.

She looked at the notebook.

"Hey!" she cried. "You wrote that down as a pro."

"It is a pro."

"I thought it was a con."

"Well, you're wrong," he smirked. "It's a great thing to have different experiences of life."

"I guess," she relented.

He continued the list of pros by noting their shared love of Hitchcock, Thai food and working with their hands. Within a couple of minutes, the pros could no longer fit on the page while the con side still only had one point.

"And there we have it," he said playfully, holding up the list. "An overwhelming argument in favor of kissing."

It was impossible to not be charmed by David and Nadine stopped trying. She shook her head at him as if to suggest that at a different moment in time, perhaps when she was not under his spell, she might be able to create a list. Clearly in his presence her mind was blank and she gently licked her lips, longing to kiss him.

She took the notebook from him and tossed it on the couch. He let her take control. She took his arms and wrapped them around her and she looked longingly into his eyes for a long time before she kissed him. The sensation was unbeatable, like sinking into a hot bath after a day in the cold. Everything about their connection was perfect. She pressed herself up against him. His body fit hers. His scent aroused her. The feeling of the skin on the back of his neck beneath her fingers was divine. He was so sexy to her. Their undeniable physical chemistry was so profound that it felt as though the world around her disappeared completely when they were together. It was as though they existed together in a bubble, just the two of them.

She longed to be naked with him. She wanted him to take her and have his way with her. The ache of her longing overwhelmed her. An hour or so later, she knew she had to either send him home or take him to her bedroom, but her conscience wasn't ready to accept their co-written pro-con list as an argument. She opted to bid him goodnight.

* * * *

Nadine got to the lounge earlier than she had expected. She was seated at a table for two in the window and took the opportunity to examine herself in her compact. Though she had the beginnings of some faint laugh lines, she really looked the same as she had when she'd been David's age. She applied a sheer peach colored lip gloss that accentuated the coral dress she wore. She'd put her hair up in rollers so that it was full of body and cascaded over her shoulders, exactly as she'd wanted. Good hair days felt like little signs from the universe that everything would work out. She hadn't seen Marnie in a few weeks and she was looking forward to telling her about her biggest sale to date.

Before Marnie had even sat down, before she'd even taken off her coat, she said, "So tell me about the boy toy."

Nadine got up to hug her friend. "There's not that much to tell. Hi," she said. Marnie's immediacy was jarring. Nadine couldn't help but notice that she seemed like an addict looking for a fix.

"Whatever," Marnie said, as she sat down and flagged the server over. "Spill it, sister."

"Hey, ladies," the server said. "Can I get you started with a drink? We've got Bellinis on special."

"Great. Two of those," Marnie said.

Nadine took Marnie's ordering as a gesture that suggested dominance, but she wasn't sure she was ready to submit to her friend's curiosity.

"So…" Marnie smiled. "What's going on?"

Nadine was not used to being the one with the latest gossip. It had been fun to tell Marnie about David back when he'd been just an abstract idea — some young hot guy who worked with her, who accepted her orders with enthusiasm. It had even been fun when they'd joked about her little boy toy, but now that she had developed real feelings for him, she wanted to protect David from Marnie's scrutiny. Or maybe it was herself she wanted to protect. She wasn't sure.

"You first," she said.

"Fine," Marnie scoffed in a joking way. "Let's see. Well, Tracy's finally pregnant. The IVF worked. Maybe she'll have twins."

Marnie's idea of news usually involved other people's news before her own. She gave updates of everyone at the office before finally sharing the news that was relevant to her. "And I found out that Cameron and his girlfriend moved in together."

"Oh no," Nadine said, remembering what a mess Marnie was after she and Cameron broke up. "How are you handling it?"

"It's fine. I mean, I heard they're getting a dog and trying for a baby. So, good for them. I'm over it." Marnie's tone was unconvincing but Nadine respected that Marnie was trying to tell herself a new story. After months of scowling or crying whenever anyone made mention of Cameron, Marnie's delivery of this news was surprisingly unemotional.

"Well, good. You were never a dog person or a baby person, for that matter, so yeah, it's probably for the best."

The Bellinis arrived and the two friends clinked glasses. Marnie took a big sip.

"It sucks," she said. "Who am I kidding? I hope I never run into them when they're out with the dog or baby or whatever." She shook her head. "Gross."

Nadine nodded.

"Like, who does he think he's kidding? He cheated on me with that whore and now she's going to have his baby? He's totally going to cheat on her later. That's so messed up."

Nadine did not like that Marnie referred to Cameron's girlfriend as a whore, but she knew Marnie was still teeming with sadness. She put her hand on Marnie's arm.

"You'll be okay," she said. "Cameron never really understood you, and you deserve to find someone who does."

"I know. I know." Marnie seemed impatient. "Anyway, tell me about the boy toy."

"Well, *David*" — she emphasized his name — "David is so sweet. I'm really charmed by him."

"Have you used him for sex yet?"

"No!" Nadine was indignant. "I don't think I could. I really don't."

"Oh, why not? Alfonso is totally right about this. He's into being used, you know."

"You don't know him."

"I saw him that time at the bookstore."

"*One* time," Nadine said.

"They're running wild with hormones at that age. Sexual peak."

"Do we really need to get into stereotypes? I'm telling you, there's something else going on. We've got this…connection."

"Did you at least make out?"

Nadine nodded and turned the color of her dress. Her skin betrayed her body's desires.

"Shut up!" Marnie clapped her hands together like this was the best possible news. "Tell me everything."

"He has lips like you would not believe. And he's super built. He took me in his arms and I just, like" — she shook her head in disbelief — "I melted."

"Mmmm. You are one smitten kitten."

"I am, I'm afraid."

"Oh, so what. Worse things have happened. Have your fun with him. What could possibly go wrong?"

"I have so much on the line right now with this business."

"All the more reason to blow off some steam."

"I guess."

"You deserve it, Nadine. I think this is the universe's way of rewarding you for getting here. I mean, it's a big deal what you're doing, taking a huge leap of faith career wise and after all that bullshit with Allan..."

"Well, that's the strange part. I feel like David and I have more in common than I had with him. Maybe I'm supremely immature when it comes down to it."

"Maybe. So what?"

"You're right."

A couple of Bellinis later, Marnie had pretty much succeeded in convincing Nadine that all of her insecurities stemmed from societal expectations and stupid things that boiled down to conformity.

"Just because he's younger doesn't mean anything," Nadine slurred. "I mean, I should count myself lucky. And hey, when I'm ninety and he's seventy-nine, he can be the one who goes to the drugstore for us."

"Now you're talking." Marnie sipped up the last of her drink with a straw, made a slurping sound and they both cracked up. The night was officially over. They took cabs home.

* * * *

From the safety of her bedroom—dressed in her white camisole with lace trim and her matching lace panties—Nadine did the one thing she had told herself never to do. She drunk-called David. When she'd told Marnie earlier that she was actually pretty immature, she'd had an image of herself doing this very thing. It was precisely the kind of thing one did in one's early twenties, but not at her age.

"What are you doing?" she asked, trying to sound casual.

"Uh, it's midnight." David sounded surprised. After a pause, he asserted, "I was fantasizing about you."

"You were?" Nadine purred into the phone.

"Yeah. I was wondering what you're wearing right now."

"Naughty boy," she said in a semi-scold. "Lace."

"Oh really," he said. "What color?"

"White."

"Oh my God."

"You like white lace?"

"Um, yeah. That's totally the Victoria's Secret catalog dream come true."

"Oh really?"

David gulped. "Nadine, you are the sexiest woman I've ever met."

"Oh yeah?"

"Oh yeah," he said in his most manly voice. "You drive me wild."

"Will I see you soon?"

"Any time," he said. "How about this weekend?"

"Sure."

"Let me take you out. On a real date."

"What's a real date?" she asked flirtatiously.

"It's where we do something to try to distract ourselves from our true desire."

"Oh? What's our true desire?" Nadine adjusted her seat. She was on her bed and lay back and got comfortable.

"I think you know."

"Tell me." Nadine had no idea just how badly her coquettish side wanted out.

"Nadine Baxter, I want to explore every inch of you with my mouth. I want to lick your nipples and suck on them until you beg me for more. Then I want to unlock your mysteries and figure out exactly what makes you moan."

Nadine's pussy was throbbing with lust. She didn't know what to say. This was not a boy on the phone. This was definitely a man. This was *the* man she had been waiting her entire life to meet. He was here now.

"Are you still there?" David asked.

"Um," she trembled. "That was the hottest thing I've ever heard. You have yourself a date. When are you picking me up?"

"How about Saturday evening at six?"

"I will be ready. I'll wear lace, but you won't be able to see it."

"You're making me crazy, Nadine. I'm not going to get anything done between now and Saturday."

"Me neither."

"Goodnight, beautiful goddess."

"Goodnight."

Chapter Twelve

Nadine was left wanting more, a lot more. The days trickled by slowly, ever so slowly. The torture! She was hot for David, yet there was still that shrinking part of her that was concerned about getting involved with someone she was pretty sure she couldn't be with in the long run. How could she introduce him to her family? What would she say if they ran into her old colleagues? Yet, the more she thought about it, the more it irked her to cling to society's expectations. After all, she wasn't interested in marriage anymore. It had been too painful to watch how her own parents and aunts and grandparents had suffered through the institution, and she didn't exactly need a man. After what Allan had done to her, she didn't want to risk having a husband, just in case he left. She was a modern woman, doing everything on her own, including paying for her beautiful home and this new business that she felt passionate about.

In the olden days, women had to choose men who were good providers, but she had the freedom to love whomever she wanted. There was really no reason not to indulge a little. Besides, when was the last time she'd really kicked back and enjoyed herself? For that matter, when was the last time she'd had sex?

The week went by quickly. She delivered the two pieces of refinished furniture on Tuesday after work, much to the satisfaction of the buyer. She got an impressive paycheck for her efforts and it was satisfying to deposit it into her business account, which was starting to look sizeable. The woman who'd bought the furniture was so thrilled, she asked Nadine to take a look at some picture frames and a sideboard from the old country that needed refurbishing. Nadine decided to take on the work and the two women shook on a great price.

She made herself an appointment at the estheticians. It was time to reward herself. It had been ages since she'd had a proper treatment—full leg wax with a French bikini line and a pedicure to boot. Manicures weren't practical in her line of work. Besides, she preferred the way her hands looked without polish. She also got a facial and the young woman who did the treatment gave such a great massage that Nadine's willpower went out of the window and she left the day spa with some semi-permanent lashes as well. It was great fun to remember that she actually did have a sex kitten side to herself.

By the time Saturday came around, Nadine figured that she had earned herself a perfectly relaxing day off. She slept in and went about her morning in the most glorious way—with coffee and a croissant in bed curled up with the Saturday paper. She did the crossword until well after noon.

* * * *

David's week had also been busy. He'd written a paper on Nietzsche's appreciation of Dostoyevsky and he'd contemplated and annotated Hannah Arendt's essays in preparation for his next paper. Philosophy left him no time for goofy fun with his roommates, though they did all share a beer on Friday night.

"Hey, you remember the bookstore manager I told you about?" David asked.

"The hot one?"

"Yeah."

"What about her?" Chris wanted to know.

"I'm taking her out."

"Dude. What?"

"Yeah. It's happening."

"Are you going to bring her here?"

"To this frat house? I'm trying my best not to."

Chris nodded. "Probably for the best. Most chicks don't understand this kind of thing." He gestured to the pile of empties that had piled up over the course of the month. With three beer-drinkers in the household, there was an abundance of cans each week.

In between classes and reading, David had thought about where to take the beautiful goddess. He'd figured that she wouldn't be expecting much in the way of fanciness. She'd seen his car, and although she hadn't seen his place yet, she could probably guess that a first year university guy's place that he shared with two other dudes wouldn't exactly be all that nice. And although he'd made some better fashion choices as of late, there was no way that she would be expecting to be taken for some kind of super swanky date. Also, David was not interested in hiding his disdain for ridiculous expressions of class privilege. He preferred a more humble approach to life and if she really liked him, he figured, she'd appreciate his taste.

* * * *

It was a fine fall evening when David picked Nadine up. The air was crisp and cool, but it wasn't cold. David fidgeted with his keys in his pocket on his way to knock at the front door.

Nadine opened the door to reveal pure radiance. It was almost as though she was glowing and David felt his knees buckle beneath him, like he had experienced in fourth grade when Cindy Turlington agreed to be his Valentine. He'd fretted and fussed over asking her and when she said yes, he realized that he didn't know what came next and he fainted. He wouldn't faint this time. No, he'd step up.

"Nadine, you are breathtaking tonight," he said, giving her an innocent kiss.

Nadine pulled him in and kissed him in a way that said she was not expecting this night to be chaste and sweet. David was caught off guard by her forceful nature, but he loved it. He pressed his lips to hers and wrapped his arms around her. How he adored holding her like this. Their bodies fit together in a way that felt like they were made for each other. He didn't want to get ahead of himself by pointing it out. After all, it was true what Nick had said—that it wasn't good to go too fast too soon. Better to let her come to him, which was precisely what this moment was all about. She was coming to him. She expressed her desire with the kiss. David's nerves disappeared.

"Would you like to come in for a glass of something before we go?" Nadine said.

"I would love a glass of something later," David said. "But I've planned some stuff for us, so I'd be happy to get going."

"Oh." Nadine's eyes lit up. "Great. I'll get my jacket."

They stepped down her stairs hand in hand. David unlocked the passenger side of the car, opened it for Nadine and waited for her to have her seatbelt fastened before he closed the door.

When he got in the car on the other side and saw the vision of Nadine Baxter in his car, right there beside him, he was again overcome by excitement. He couldn't help but want to kiss her sensual lips again. He resisted. *Let her come to you*, he remembered Nick saying.

"Okay, so I have kind of a crazy evening planned. There are some friends I want to introduce you to." He smiled. "I was hoping you wouldn't mind if we bring them along on our date."

"Oh, uh, okay," Nadine said, sounding polite.

"They're really going to appreciate it. They don't get out much, and nothing like what we're about to do tonight."

David knew it was a strange plan to spring on Nadine, especially considering that it was their first official date, but he needed her to know that this was the kind of guy he was. David pulled into the SPCA parking lot. Theirs was the only car in there.

"I think it's closed," Nadine said.

"I have a key," David explained. "I'm one of their head volunteers. I've been doing this since I was fifteen."

"So, wait a second. The friends that are coming on our date are animals?"

"Yeah." David smiled. "Dogs. Specifically Duchess and Duke."

Nadine laughed her head off. "You're hilarious," she said. "Just when I was thinking this is getting pretty weird. I was wondering who these friends of yours are."

"Furry ones."

Nadine laughed again. "I can't wait to meet Duchess and Duke."

"Oh, good." David grinned. "They're excited about meeting you, too. I told them all about you."

"Should I come in with you?"

"No, it's best not to. You have to disinfect your shoes and go through this whole procedure. Plus, it's hard on the dogs to see people at night. They get all excited. It makes me feel bad because we can't take them all out, right? I already prepared the gang for this."

"You talk to dogs?"

"Sure. Why not?"

* * * *

It was David's goofy grin that melted Nadine's heart. She had never been on a date like this before and they were only getting started. She waited in the car and checked her lips in the passenger side mirror. Should she wear lip gloss? She wanted to send the sign that it was okay to kiss when the mood struck. She dabbed a tiny bit on.

David emerged with a beautiful and graceful Irish Setter and a somewhat scruffy-looking Black Labrador. He looked happy to be with them. His friends. It was as though there were three tails wagging instead of two. Nadine giggled at the sight and opened her door.

"Who's who?" she asked.

"This is Duchess," David said of the Irish Setter. "She's four. And this is Duke."

Nadine put her hand down and let the dogs sniff her before she gave them each a scratch behind the ear.

David opened the trunk of his station wagon, spread out a thick blanket and let the dogs hop in. They panted in excitement. David closed the back door and walked around to the driver's side.

"Where are you taking us?" Nadine wanted to know.

"It's a surprise. It's a bit of a drive, but like I said, Duchess and Duke don't get out much so this'll do them a world of good."

"What's their story?"

"It's kind of sad, actually. Are you sure you want to know?"

"Yeah."

"Well, Duchess is Duke's best friend in the whole world. They've been inseparable since Duchess was just a pup. Duke was already ten then."

"So he's fourteen?"

"Yeah. And their owner is a lovely woman, Mrs. Bronstein, but she's just been moved to a nursing home and they won't allow dogs. Sometimes they take little dogs, but Duchess and Duke were too big."

"So they're here?"

"Mrs. Bronstein's kids couldn't take them."

"That's so sad."

"There's more."

"Oh no."

"I don't have to tell you. I don't want to make you sad. I just thought it'd be nice for us to do something good for Duchess and Duke tonight."

"I want to know."

"Okay, well, Duke has cancer."

"Oh no." Nadine began to tear up. She looked back at the two of them, where they lay all cozy and looking out of the window together. Their affection for each other was obvious.

"Yeah, this is his last night."

"You mean?"

David nodded. He also had a tear in his eye. "That's why I thought it'd be nice to let them have a really special evening with us."

Nadine turned into a giant mush ball. "Can't anything be done?"

"Not at this point. It has spread too much. Besides, there's no one to pay for the chemo. Mrs. Bronstein has her own health problems to worry about."

"Doesn't it make you sad to volunteer for the SPCA?" Nadine asked.

"No, it feels good to know I'm part of something bigger than myself. These dogs are pure love and joy. I mean, just look at Duke. He knows what's going to happen tomorrow. You think he lets that ruin his day? No."

Nadine looked at Duke. His tongue was hanging out of his mouth and he was panting and enjoying the view.

"He's a strong spirit," Nadine said.

David nodded. "I have learned so much from my friends over the years."

"What's going to happen to Duchess?"

"I'm not too worried about her. Look at how charming and beautiful she is. She'll find someone who will love her back in no time."

"You're so confident. I heard that adult dogs have a hard time getting adopted."

"Some do. Duchess won't. Just wait until you see her in action on the mountain."

"Mountain?"

"We're going up to Potawatomi Trail for an evening hike."

"But I'm not wearing proper footwear."

"Trust me. It's not so bad. It's a wheelchair accessible hike. Duke can't handle much in the way of hills, but he's gonna love the view from up there. I think you will, too."

"David, this is really sweet and not at all what I was expecting."

"What were you expecting?"

"I really had no idea."

"Good." He grabbed her hand and gave it a squeeze. "I don't want you to have expectations. It's better to be open-minded."

* * * *

The air was chilly and Nadine felt a breeze tickle her cheeks as she stepped out into the evening. While David ran around back and got Duchess and Duke outfitted in their leashes, Nadine thought of Grandpa Winston and the sweetness and preciousness of life.

"Here," David said, passing her the leashes. "Hold these for just a second."

He whipped around the car, locking the back door to the trunk and opening the back seat door. He lifted out a backpack and put it on, then he came back and put his hand out for the leashes. "Do you want to take one? You don't have to."

"I'd love to."

"Which one?"

"I don't know."

"All right. Close your eyes." She followed the instructions. "And open them." She did.

David's eyes were still closed. He'd taken one leash from her. "All right!" he said, opening his eyes. "It's you and me, Duke," he said to the dog. "We're about to have the best night of your life. You ready, boy?"

The dog wagged his tail. David took him into his arms and explained that he probably shouldn't exert himself too much on the trail, but he could run around a little once they were up top.

Nadine looked at Duchess. Her big brown eyes made Nadine feel so warm inside, in spite of the slight temperature drop with the increase in elevation.

"Duchess doesn't need a leash," David said. "You can take it off her if you want."

"What? Really? What if she doesn't listen to me?"

"She will."

"But..."

"You don't have to, but I think you'll be impressed with her. She's so incredibly well trained. Mrs. Bronstein worked with her from the time she was born, and she used to be a professional trainer."

"No kidding." Nadine shook her head. "How do you know all this?"

"I always get the whole story when I do intake. It's important to know the history of the dog in case there's been any abuse or whatnot. I know, it's not nice to think about, but not all dogs have great lives and it really affects the kinds of homes they should go to. Duchess here can go anywhere."

He scratched Duchess on the head and reached into his pocket and pulled out a couple of Milk-Bones. "Check this out."

Both dogs sat down in anticipation.

"Duke, lie down." Duke did. "Sit up." He did. "Speak." Duke barked. "Now sing!"

Duke let out a long series of howls and David tossed him the treat, which he caught with his mouth.

"Now, Duchess, you get to really show off what you can do." David put the Milk-Bone behind his ear and held his hands out. "Duchess, dance."

Duchess jumped up on her hind legs and did a pirouette in front of them. Nadine almost couldn't believe it, but Duchess wasn't finished. She rested her paws on David's palms and they did a type of two-step around the parking lot. David tossed the treat to Duchess. Nadine laughed so hard. This was the most amazing sight she'd ever seen.

"Incredible! I'm almost jealous," she said.

"Is that so? Would you care for a dance?"

David gestured for Nadine to take his hands. "Duke and Duchess, sit!" he ordered and they obeyed. Then David and Nadine two-stepped. Duchess barked. Nadine cracked up.

David said, "I think I know who's jealous."

The gang took the path marked with a sign that pointed out a scenic area ahead. Walking in silence with their two furry companions, Nadine felt an overwhelming sense of peace come over her. It was as though this moment was utterly complete, like she could think of nothing more that could possibly enhance it.

Then they arrived at the viewpoint and saw the glimmering city lights below. Her tummy, filled with butterflies, told her that this was all too much. It was like she was floating.

"David, this is amazing. I'm having the best time."

"Just wait."

"What? There's more?"

"A little something."

He opened the backpack and took out a Thermos. "I made you my famous hot chocolate."

"Oh my God."

If there was one thing that could have improved on the magic of the moment, this was it. And she saw that David was the kind of guy who really thought of everything. He opened the spout and poured some hot chocolate into the lid of the Thermos, which also functioned as a cup.

"Sorry. We're going to have to share," he said. "So you'll have to stay close to me."

"I don't mind." Nadine couldn't conceal her smile.

He passed her the cup and she got a whiff of the chocolate-y goodness. "Wait just a second," he said and dug into the backpack. He pulled out a little plastic container, opened it and sprinkled a few mini marshmallows into the cup. "All right, now try it."

She lifted the cup to her lips and was instantly transported to heaven. The flavor of dark chocolate with a creamy hint of cinnamon swirled around her palate and tasted so good.

"Whoa. This is seriously the best hot chocolate I've ever had."

David nodded humbly. "It's from scratch. I grated Bernard Callebaut dark chocolate into some organic homogenized milk."

"Wow."

Nadine had never before experienced real hot chocolate. This was a first. It was also a first that such a gorgeous guy made something like this happen for her. It was without a doubt one of the kindest gestures she'd ever experienced.

"You're romantic," she said. "This place is astounding."

"I wanted to do something you'd remember."

"David, it's incredible."

"I wanted you to know how much this night matters to me. I've been looking forward to bringing you here ever since that day you put the coffee in front of me."

"I'm so glad I did that."

"Were you trying to say something with it?"

"I just thought it'd be a nice thing to do for someone on his first day of the big rush."

"I wasn't the only one there that day. A lot of guys were having their first day."

"Okay. Fine. I thought you were cute. But, I didn't think we'd be sitting here together. So, no, I wasn't hitting on you or anything. I figured you were way too young and wouldn't go for someone like me."

"What? Someone like you? You mean the beautiful goddess? Nadine, you have to know that any guy would go for you. You're, like, universally sexy. Tell me you know that."

"I don't think of myself that way."

He shook his head. "I guess that's the paradox. That's what makes you so damned sexy."

She smiled. "You really think so?"

"Nadine." He shook his head and didn't say anything. He grabbed her and pulled her in close and kissed her. It was passionate abandon and she did not want to let go this time. She needed him to know that she was attracted to him. There was no reason to conceal this from him, no reason at all.

"This is easily the best date I've ever been on," Nadine said.

"I'm glad. I wasn't sure if you'd be okay with the simple things, you know."

"I love this, David." She gestured out at the breathtaking vista. "I mean, it's absolutely romantic."

He looked shy for a minute. "I love simple things. That's the kind of person I am. I figured I could take you to a trendy restaurant or something, but it'd be misleading, because that's not the kind of place I like to go. I come up here quite a bit, to tell the truth, though never with a date, not even the furry kind."

Nadine laughed at his joke. But she really enjoyed the image of a guy who came up here by himself.

"What do you do up here?" she wanted to know. "Drink hot chocolate?"

"Not usually. By myself, just tea. I come up here to think. I do a lot of thinking."

"Philosophy?"

"Yeah. Meaning of life. That sort of thing. Kind of a natural reaction to death, I suppose."

"Oh, David. Who?"

"My parents. My brother."

"David," Nadine whispered. She didn't know what to say except his name.

"It's okay. I've made peace with it. I know they're out there, you know. I can feel them when I come up here."

Nadine had tears in her eyes. How she ever could have misjudged David was beyond her. He was an old soul and that was as clear as the crisp night sky.

"When did you lose them?"

"A few years ago now. My senior year. Car accident. Instant."

"Oh, David. That must have been so hard."

"It was." He looked out at the skyline as though for a second he was far away. Then he took another sip of hot chocolate and smiled at Nadine. "But you know what I realized?"

"What?"

"That there were two ways to go through life. I could either feel sorry for myself or I could let myself feel the pain of loss and move forward with all the love that I still feel for them. I chose the latter. My grandparents helped. They are amazing. I'd like you to meet them."

"Sure. I'd love to." Nadine was surprised to hear the words come out of her mouth so quickly and enthusiastically on the first date.

"They'll like you a lot. I'm sure."

Nadine smiled at the thought. "Did you live with them after?"

"I did. It wasn't a big change, since they already lived downstairs. We did some rearranging that year and moved them upstairs and I took their old suite and we remodeled and repainted, just to sort of change up the energy, you know?"

"That makes sense."

"They're such strong souls. It really helped me to watch them deal with everything. It wasn't easy for them to lose their only son." He looked out over the horizon again.

Nadine could tell it was hard for him to share so much with her.

"But they have such strong faith, you know. It's really amazing. My grandmother says we're all eternal beings, and there is no real beginning or end to life. Things just change form."

"That's a good way to look at it," Nadine said. She took his arm and looped her own in it. She rested her head on his shoulder.

"Life is about savoring each moment. That's what I believe. So I try to surround myself with beauty as much as I can, and I try not to dwell on bad stuff or spend time doing anything I'm not sincerely passionate about."

"That makes so much sense," Nadine said. "We have to enjoy life."

She thought back to her previous hesitations about David based on shallow surface things like age and income difference, and she made peace with her choice right then and there. She was passionate about him. She loved being here with him in this moment and, after all, that was the whole point and the only thing that mattered.

"Speaking of enjoying life, I brought something else along, too."

He dug into his backpack again and pulled out a big container. When he opened the lid, Nadine saw cut up pieces of meat.

"Steak," David said. "Nothing but the best for Duke."

Nadine started to cry. She was overwhelmed with the generosity of David's spirit. To think that he wanted to give Duke such a great night and that he could do it with such grace. She wiped her eyes with her fingers, not wanting to be overly emotional.

"It's okay," he said, wiping her cheek with his thumb. "Look at the joy in this moment. That's what we have. Right now. Look at Duke. Look how happy he is."

He passed the container to her. "Here. You first."

Nadine took a piece of steak out of the container and Duke and Duchess immediately sat down.

"I don't want to make him do a trick for it," Nadine said.

"Why not? He wants to. He's a showoff. Get him to shake a paw."

"Okay." She had tears in her eyes as she gave the command. She gave Duke the morsel and watched as he devoured it. Her heart filled with love.

"I have to capture this," David said and whipped out his cell phone camera. "Don't worry about me. Just do whatever comes naturally."

She nodded.

She had a dance with Duchess and got Duke to speak. Nadine rewarded them with more chunks of the good stuff and the dogs loved it. They'd been plenty happy before, but they were ecstatic now. It was obvious.

Chapter Thirteen

Back in the car heading toward the city, Nadine decided to say the one thing she'd been thinking all evening that she couldn't say before.

"David?"

"Yes?"

"I'd like to adopt Duchess."

David pulled over onto the shoulder of the road. He turned and looked at her, warmly but with the kind of skepticism of everyone at the SPCA.

"Adopting a dog is a huge decision."

"I know."

"And you didn't wake up this morning thinking you wanted a dog, so I don't know if it's such a good idea. I mean, of course it's easy to fall in love with a dog like Duchess, but loving her isn't enough. It's a lot of work. You work full-time and you're running the business. I don't know. I mean, I don't want to be negative but…"

"David, I understand your defensiveness, but I've been thinking about getting a dog for a while, actually."

"You have?"

She nodded. "It's not a split second decision. Actually, I already know for a fact I can bring her to work with me."

"She'd like that," he conceded.

"Yeah, and as for the business, Grandpa Winston had a dog in his shop. I'm not totally there yet. I'm still working out of a storage space, but I'm looking at commercial spaces. I'll get there within the year, I'm sure. Then I'll go down to part-time at the store until I'm sure I can stay ahead of my bills."

"Whoa, Nadine. I had no idea."

"About what?"

"All your plans. That's really cool that you want a commercial space."

"Well, I can't keep working out of my garage forever. Oh, and get this. I made two huge sales this week after I delivered the dresser on Tuesday. It's picking up. I can feel it."

"Wow. That's so exciting. I'm proud of you."

"So what do you think about Duchess? I mean, I know the timing isn't totally ideal, but I feel like she's the perfect dog for me."

"I can see why. Two beauties. Don't feel like you have to, though, just because I told you their sob story. Every dog I know has one."

"David. It's not the story. It's her. I really click with her."

"She sure would benefit from going to a loving home before her best friend... You know..."

"I guess that is a part of it. I can't bear the thought of her in an empty kennel after Duke..."

"But that's no reason to take her."

"It's not the reason. It's just how I know I love her."

"Oh, Nadine. That's such a beautiful thing to say."

"It's the truth."

"Well, listen. Let's drop them off tonight and I'll leave a note for Shirley, who'll do up the paperwork in the morning. Then we can make sure you're all set up to take her." He looked back out at the city, now closer because they'd come back from the trail. "Whoa. I can't believe you're going to take Duchess. You are my dream woman. I'd have taken her myself if I could. I didn't want Duchess to have to live with a bunch of guys. It wasn't right for her. She's so classy."

"You love her, too."

"Sure do. Dogs like Duchess don't come around very often. I don't mean that as a bad reflection on the other dogs. It's just that she's exceptional."

"Yeah. She really is." Nadine looked back at Duchess and smiled at the idea of bringing a dog back into her life. "You know, my grandfather used to have a dog like her."

"Oh yeah?"

Nadine nodded. "Yeah. He taught me everything I know about it, actually."

"No kidding."

"Yep. And I used to just love going to his shop after school and on weekends to see him and to spend time with Buddy. Buddy was a boy. I'm kind of excited to have a girl dog."

"What happened to Buddy?" David asked. Nadine had a feeling he would. It had, after all, been a sore point all these years and this was the perfect time to share it.

"Well, after Grandpa Winston passed away, I wanted to take Buddy, but I wasn't in the right frame of mind. Everything in my life had just collapsed."

"Rough," David said taking her hand.

"Yeah. My parents sold off his shop so quickly that I barely even had a chance to adjust to the idea. It was gone almost as soon as they put it on the market. He had such a great reputation. It's still a furniture restoration place, actually. Anyway, Buddy went to a new home and I was all excited because the new family said I could come visit him any time, but then they moved a little farther away and I called them about coming out, and they didn't have time."

"That must have been hard on you."

"It was. Truth be told, it took me a long time to forgive my parents. I can see now that they were busy with their careers and responsibilities, but the whole experience felt so abrupt and cold."

"Understandable. I'm really glad you feel comfortable enough to tell me about this."

"Well, you shared."

"I feel like I can tell you anything."

"It's mutual," Nadine said. "David, you know you really don't strike me as being much younger than me."

"Phew. I take that as a huge compliment. I was worried that you couldn't see yourself with me."

There was an awkward silence for a second while Nadine digested what David had just said.

As though he was uncomfortable with the silence, David added, "I mean, you don't have to see yourself with me at all. I'm…uh… Oh crap. I was doing my best not to come on too strong."

Nadine looked at David's hand, which still rested on hers. She looked into his eyes.

"You were? I thought you were all about being yourself completely tonight."

"Well, I am. But I still find it hard to believe I'm out with you, so I've been trying to play it cool."

"You have?" She smiled. It was impossible not to.

"You couldn't tell?" He shook his fist in the air while looking out of the window. "Oh, man. I knew it wasn't working."

"You're wearing your heart on your sleeve, David, and I have to say it is so refreshing."

"It is?"

"Oh yes."

"So you can accept that I'm kind of a schmaltzy guy who likes to hang out with dogs and drink hot chocolate?"

"I think you're incredibly sweet."

"Oh no. Sweet. The kiss of death."

"Not in my book."

"When a girl says you're sweet, it means she just wants to hang out and make cookies together."

"Cookies?"

"Tamara Sanders. Freshman year. I was head over heels and she said she liked me too then she invited me over to her place and I thought it was a date, but turned out she just wanted advice from a guy's perspective on how to get Jared Blackley."

"Ugh. Why do they always have names like Jared?"

"Who?"

"Those perfect high school dudes."

"Tell me about it. We made cookies and did *Cosmo* quizzes, and it sucked."

"I wonder where Jared is today."

"Actually they got married. He was all right, as it turned out. I went to their wedding. Told the cookie story. Got some laughs and a pinch on the cheek from Tamara's mom."

David rubbed his cheek like he was remembering. "It hurts being the sweet guy."

"Well, you sure weren't sweet the other night on the phone," Nadine said. Even in the relative darkness of the car, she was embarrassed, as she could feel herself blush at the memory.

* * * *

David pulled the car into the SPCA parking lot. The evening had grown dark in that way that is common in Michigan.

"Can't we do anything about Duke?" Nadine wanted to know.

"You mean to prevent the inevitable?"

She nodded.

He told her there was nothing left to be done and when he got the black Lab out of the car and held Duke in his arms, he carried him to Nadine.

"Feel here," he said, putting her hand in his and guiding it to a lump on Duke's left hip. "That's just one of the tumors. There are more."

Nadine began to cry.

"I know it's awfully selfish of me," she said, "but I want him to live. I want him to beat this." It sounded naïve, even as she said it, especially considering that David had lost his whole family. She felt silly for pointing out the powerlessness in the situation.

"We have to approach this the way Duke is," David said. "Look. You don't see him getting all gloomy."

Duke was, in fact, wagging his tail.

"He's had a great night," Nadine said, as though she was making an effort to console herself.

"I'm going to take him in and have a minute with him," David said. "I'll be back for Duchess in a bit."

"All right." She nodded.

In the parking lot, Nadine let Duchess out of the car. The Irish Setter jumped out, tail wagging and eager. David was right. She was beautiful. She probably could have been a show dog with her silky mahogany coat. Nadine looked into Duchess' eyes and wondered if she knew what the morning would bring.

"I want you to know you have a home with me, Duchess," she told the dog. "I will look after you and care for you, just like Grandpa Winston did for Buddy. We're going to have a great time together, you and me."

Duchess shifted her weight from one side of her seated position to the other and stared back at Nadine.

"We're going to go running every morning. I can't wait to show you the trails by the house."

It was like having a new friend — a best friend — and she needed Duchess more than she could even express. Lately, her friends had put pressure on her to make more time for them and to live a more balanced life, but Nadine had goals and plans. What she didn't have was time. Duchess would force her out into the fresh air each day and the run would do her good. Then they'd go to work and it'd be easier to get through the day with her friend at her feet.

Just then, David emerged from the building and in the shadows beneath the canopy of oak trees, Nadine noticed that his eyes were red.

"Let's give them their last night together," David said, holding his hand out for Duchess' leash.

"Come on, Duchess," David called, and Duchess ran to him with such enthusiasm that Nadine wondered if she'd listen to anyone. But she understood that Duchess was confused. Life in the shelter was undoubtedly stressful for all dogs being housed there. She probably missed Mrs. Bronstein and was trying to impress everyone in an effort to get back to her. She knew that visits to see Mrs. Bronstein would be in their future.

"Take good care, Duchess," Nadine called to her. "I'll see you tomorrow."

* * * *

Nadine noticed that this time, when David came out, he looked at peace. It was a relief to see, as she really didn't like to see him suffer. It had bothered her more than she'd thought it would. She couldn't believe that this was their first real date. They seemed to know each other so well.

"Hey," he said as he stepped into the light of the street lamp from above. "Thank you for meeting my friends."

She was still outside the car, leaning up against it in the cool evening air. She put her arms around him. "It was a pleasure to meet your friends."

"I hope I didn't bum you out with Duke."

"I am sad, but you're right about death. People – and dogs – don't disappear, they just change forms. I'm grateful that I met Duke. He's a special dog."

"He is. He has had a dream life. It's pointless to make him suffer through all kinds of horrible operations that would prevent him from running and playing and enjoying himself. I'm so glad you get me and get my love for this place."

"Oh, David, I do."

Nadine examined him with unmistakable compassion in this difficult moment, but there was something else in her eye contact, too. It was a deep longing, an uncontrollable magnetism.

In the dark parking lot, beneath the street lamp, shaded by oak leaves, they kissed. David initiated it but Nadine kept it going longer than David had anticipated. Nadine's urge to kiss him had started around the time he came to her door and it had built consistently for the past two hours. Now she wasn't willing to wait longer. She wanted more of him. She was able to give in completely

When they finally tore themselves apart, David said, "I have more planned for us."

"There's more? Really?" Nadine was delighted, but also felt a twinge of disappointment that it wasn't time to go back to her place yet. She sure wanted more of this physical expression. She was able to tell him with her kiss what she couldn't seem to say in words.

"I want to show you something," David said as they pulled out of the parking lot. "It's another one of my happy places, but it's happy for different reasons."

"Oh yeah?"

"It's another place I like to go a lot. I'm there at least one night a week, but usually there are others there, too. Tonight it'll just be the two of us."

"How mysterious."

"Yeah. And you can't tell people. We have special permission for just tonight. I prearranged it."

"Where are you taking me?"

"Do you want to know? I can tell you if you do, but I was going to surprise you."

"Okay, surprise me." Nadine looked out of the window.

Before long they were in a neighborhood she didn't usually come to. David drove through the streets like a pro. It was easy to see that he felt comfortable here. Nadine's voice was low, like she was reluctant to say anything. "David, you're really romantic."

He glanced over to her for just a second and gave a flirtatious smile. "What did you expect?"

"I don't know."

"It's a pleasure to have the privilege of taking you out," he said.

She felt like the luckiest woman in the world. His attention was intoxicating. She put her hand on his leg as he drove. He covered her hand with his and held it there, pressing into him. She was in heaven.

They pulled into the parking lot of a strange place she hadn't been to.

"Isn't this a museum?"

"Yep. And planetarium."

"But it's closed."

"To the public." He grinned.

"What?"

"I told you. You can't tell anyone. This is a special privilege."

"We're not breaking in, are we?"

"Would that be romantic? Getting a criminal record together?" His smile was playful and Nadine felt foolish for blurting out the first paranoid thought that had come into her mind.

"This is an unusual date destination, you have to admit."

"I'm an unusual guy," he said.

"So I'm learning."

They walked hand in hand up the concrete steps. Nadine was surprised that she didn't feel nervous. This was fun. So far this was easily the most exciting night she'd had in ages. She'd grown accustomed to guys taking her out for the tired old dinner and movie or dinner and lounge. This was the first original date she'd been on since... Well, for as long as she could remember.

They circled around to the back of the building and climbed another flight of stairs. Then David took out a key and unlocked the door. A beeping sound followed. David bolted inside and Nadine, from outside, could hear him punch a code into the alarm. The beeping stopped. How he had managed to gain access to this place, she did not know, but it sure was thrilling. She followed him inside. There was just a tiny lamp on at the back, where they were. It felt like they had entered a dark theater after the movie had started and that an usher was lighting their steps. But then David turned on the dim overhead lights and Nadine saw that they were actually inside a massive dome.

"Whoa!" she couldn't help but exclaim. "This is incredible."

She looked up at what appeared to be the night sky, but fainter. They were inside the planetarium, a place she'd never visited before in her life.

"Just you wait," David said. "Come. We're taking the best seats in the house." David took her by the hand and guided her to a seat in the middle of the room. She took her coat off and put it on the seat next to her. There was really no reason not to spread out. It was the only time she'd ever experienced being all alone in such a huge public space. It was so strange and silent.

"I'll be right back," David said. He ran up the aisle, flicked a switch then the lights went out and, for a moment, they were in total blackness. Then the stars lit up and overhead, it was as though the night sky lit their way. It was completely unlike the real night sky, though. It was so clear.

David came back and sat down next to her. He took her hand in his as they looked up together.

"This is incredible," Nadine said.

"I thought you might like it." David leaned back and got more comfortable. He also took his coat off and he put his arm around Nadine's seat. She felt herself get tingly everywhere. It was like it was the first time a guy had ever put his arm around her.

"So you come here a lot?" she asked.

"I'm president of the astronomy club," he said. "That's why I have the key and the code. Plus, I know all the security guards. I asked if we could come here tonight and it was fine."

"Wow," Nadine said. Teasingly and flirtatiously, she turned to him and said, "I had no idea you were a nerd."

"No idea? Really?" He laughed. "Come on. What part of studying philosophy isn't nerdy?"

"You don't look like a nerd."

"I filled out. You should have seen me in high school."

"I would have loved to have seen you in high school."

"No way. A girl like you. You would not have given me the time of day."

"How do you know?"

"Trust me. I remember girls like you. I wouldn't have had the nerve to even say hi to you back then."

"Well, there you have it. That's about you, though. Not me. I'm sure I would have thought you were adorable."

"Nope, you wouldn't have. I can show you photos."

"I hope you do."

He squeezed her close to him and kissed the top of her head. It was a sweet and innocent moment, and Nadine perceived perfectly the kind of guy David had been in high school.

She looked up again. "So, president, can you point out some constellations?"

"Sure." David smiled. "This sky is actually not the sky we see outside. Right now we're looking at the southern hemisphere's sky."

"It's different?"

"Ye-eess," David said, drawing out the vowel sound. "Were you a cheerleader in high school?"

"As a matter of fact, I was," Nadine said. "But I wasn't a walking stereotype. I got good grades, and I didn't date jocks. My boyfriend was in the drama club."

David nodded knowingly. "This sky image is taken from New Zealand in January, so the constellations are different."

"Wow."

"Yeah. That's Taurus right there"—he traced the pattern with his finger—"and over there is Reticulum. And that's Mensa. Oh, and you probably recognize Orion."

"Jeez, no wonder they made you president."

"Actually, I think it's my perfect attendance record. I haven't missed a meeting yet, except for the two years I spent on the beach."

"In how long?"

"Oh, um, let's see. Eight years."

"Did you say you spent two years on the beach?"

David nodded. "After graduation."

"So, you didn't go to university right away?"

"No."

"Phew," Nadine said. "How old are you? I've been wondering."

"Twenty-one."

Nadine was relieved. At least her worst fears weren't true.

David reached into his backpack and pulled out another plastic container.

"You're like Mary Poppins," Nadine said. "What have you got there?"

"I made a couple of sandwiches. These are *bocconcini*, *prosciutto*, tomato, basil, caramelized onions and grainy mustard."

"Yum."

He smiled.

"I'm impressed." Nadine unwrapped her sandwich from the parchment paper that enveloped it. She looked at the baguette. It smelled and looked delicious.

"Incredible!"

"Glad you like it."

"You're quite the talented guy," she managed between bites.

"Thanks. I try."

The silence and awe of the overhead view allowed Nadine to probe further into what was truly on her mind. "What do you mean you spent a couple of years on the beach?"

"Well, I almost didn't graduate. After I lost my family, I couldn't concentrate and my grades dropped. I almost left high school, but my grandparents urged me not to. So I got through, but I didn't have the grades for university and I wasn't exactly motivated. So I went and lived out of my car for a while because I needed to think and clear my head. Got my grades up by doing some online courses."

"Wait, but you lived on the beach. How'd you get Internet access?"

"Libraries. I only went to town to hand in assignments and take tests. It was great, actually."

"So you lived out of your car? The same car you're driving now?"

"The one and only."

"But it's so small. I mean, for a home."

"Not really. I can stretch out in the back and I kept a cooler on the front seat and had my gas stove and all that in the back beside me."

"But where'd you cook and make coffee?"

"Picnic areas."

"Bathroom? Showers?"

"Rest stops. Community centers. The ocean."

"Wow."

"I seem like a hippie, don't I?" David asked. "Well, I'm over it now, but back then I had no idea what direction I wanted to go in. I had to figure some stuff out."

"But, how did you get by? I mean, how'd you live?"

"Oh, I made some money. No big deal. Actually I did some pretty odd stuff to get by."

Nadine shook her head. Never before had she met anyone like David. She could tell that he didn't want to talk about it and she knew that the best people could take a long time to get to know. She didn't want to push him too hard. This was, after all, their very first date. There was lots of time, she reminded herself as she leaned into his embrace and adjusted herself to the reclining seat. This was so comfortable — resting her head on David's arm — that she couldn't think of anything that'd make the moment more complete.

Chapter Fourteen

Hours later, the two arrived back at Nadine's apartment. She'd long since abandoned the vision of a tender and sweet goodnight kiss on her front steps. She'd have been deeply disappointed with a first date scene from a romantic movie. She wanted the second or third date — the one that involved inviting the guy in.

She unlocked her door and led David inside.

"Let me take your jacket," she insisted.

"Sure," he said. He followed her upstairs.

Nadine had tried to make the place cozier. There were candles set up and ready to be lit. A blanket covered the sofa and she had tidied up the magazines that otherwise littered the coffee table.

David had gone to great lengths to make sure that Nadine knew he had taken their date seriously and he could see now that she, too, had put in a great deal of effort. Like a sprite, she zipped about lighting candles and even an aromatherapy pot of essential oils. Just then, he perceived a hint of neroli and lavender. It was very sensual and it made him feel both comforted and on edge. He could tell that she had expectations, and he didn't want to disappoint. He also didn't want to overstep or move too fast. The biggest mark of success, he reminded himself, was to get a second date.

"Can I get you anything?" Nadine asked.

"Sure. What are you having?"

"I got a bottle of New Zealand wine that I absolutely adore. It's a cabernet sauvignon, but I have other stuff, too, if you'd rather."

"You got something special for us?" His face lit up. "I'll have that."

"Great. Make yourself at home. I'll be right back."

While she was in the kitchen, David took out his iPhone and plugged it into her speakers. He played Billie Holiday, figuring that a woman like Nadine would enjoy the depth and brilliance of her voice.

Nadine emerged with two oversized glasses on a tray. Next to the glasses there was a plate divided into three and in each compartment there was some kind of snack, but David couldn't make out the exact nature of the edibles in the soft light.

Nadine set the tray down and sat down next to David on the couch. She smiled at the choice of music.

"I haven't listened to her in ages."

"I hope you like it."

"Great choice. I love Billie Holiday."

Nadine tucked her legs up onto the seat. She reached for David's hand and took it in hers, guiding his arm around her. "There," she said. "I love that."

He gave her a squeeze to let her feel how badly he wanted to hold onto her. She turned to him and he didn't hesitate. He gave her a bold kiss on the mouth.

David was all over Nadine, exploring her face, the back of her neck, her creamy skin above the neckline of her shirt.

"Mmm," Nadine moaned. "I like this side of you."

David wanted to make sure that he understood exactly. "What do you mean?"

"You're so…different suddenly, like, more aggressive."

"Do you want me to ease up?"

"No, I like it."

"Good, because there are so many things I want to do to you."

"Oh good," Nadine purred. "Maybe I should take you to the bedroom."

"I'd like that," David said. "Maybe I'll take you there." And with that, he picked her up and tossed her over his shoulder as though he was a caveman dragging his lady back to his dwelling.

"Take me," she said.

"That's all I need to hear," David said. They headed to the bedroom and David skillfully navigated his way to the bed in the darkness. He avoided turning on the overhead lamp, as the sense of the moment guided him. Somehow he knew to reach down to the switch on the soft lamp that sat atop Nadine's dresser. There was a warm glow. He placed Nadine on the bed. She was still wearing her clothes, but he hoped it wouldn't be long before they were in a heap on the floor.

David took control of the situation. He surveyed the landscape of her room as he watched her with careful attention. He noticed the candles she had on her dresser and went to them. He struck a match and lit the wicks, blew out the match and placed it carefully atop the box, so as not to leave a mark on the surface. He felt, as she did, that furniture was something to be treated with respect.

David turned back to face her, his eyes as concentrated as ever. He unbuttoned his shirt.

To Nadine, it seemed like he had just come from a week out in the woods, and he had an eagerness and roughness that suggested the same. Nadine watched him as though he was her very own male stripper, her boy toy.

"Are you going to take it off?" she asked.

He pointed to the tight white shirt. "This?"

She nodded.

"Do you want me to?"

She nodded again.

"Nadine Baxter, you naughty girl. You want to check me out, don't you?"

"Oh yes." She bit her lower lip.

"All right, you asked for it." He slowly lifted the shirt up over his chiseled chest revealing an incredibly fit abdominal region. She'd seen washboard abs in magazines, but never in person—not like this. He had the body of an athlete. She'd had no idea that he was that fit. He was so nonchalant about it, so unlike most of the jock types she'd come across over the years. He had the kind of physique she imagined artists would want to sculpt. His skin was tan and looked especially alluring in the soft lighting. She couldn't wait to touch him.

He came to her without taking his eyes off of her. It was intoxicating the way he concentrated on her.

He adjusted the pillows, creating a type of reclining position for her. Then he ran his fingers over her décolletage. She touched his skin, running her fingers over his muscular upper arms and chest. This was a view she could get used to. She flushed hot with desire at the rippling textures. He was, by anyone's definition, a sexy man. But he took her hands off him and lowered them to her sides. She fell back on the cushions she was propped up on.

"Take this off," he ordered.

Nadine was surprised at the forcefulness of his tone and she loved it. She pulled the top up over her head to reveal her bra. He kissed her left shoulder and playfully, softly, took a bite into it. Then he kissed along the top of her left shoulder, around her neck and followed a path all the way to her right shoulder like he was traversing a mountain range with his lips. She shivered and felt the light tickle of his touch everywhere. He reached behind her and without waiting for help, he unclasped the back of her bra with one hand. The man had skills.

She was topless. Exposed. Still, he kept his eyes locked with hers. His hands found her C-cup breasts and held them like they were precious gifts. He was deliberate. Then he started to massage them, lightly at first. He squeezed her nipples between his thumbs and forefingers, and she found herself hungry for his touch.

"Nadine. You are so much hotter than I ever imagined." He held her nipples taut.

She moaned at the sensation that made its way straight from her nipples to her clit. She squirmed with delight. The sight of David in front of her was almost too much to take. He caressed her breasts and lowered his mouth to take a nipple into it. She savored the slow way he sucked on her, the feeling she had that he wanted more and more of her.

She touched him back, held his head between her hands, ran her fingers through his thick brown hair. He was so good looking, and it felt good to finally give in to her attraction. She'd wanted him to take her like this ever since they survived the elevator ordeal. Had she really listened to the messages her body sent, she'd have given in to her lust back then, but she was glad they had waited. It meant that she was in a heightened state now. Watching him as he seduced her by sucking on her sensitive nipples, alternating back and forth, like he was studying her reaction, was more than she ever could have anticipated. She let herself relax into it. He signaled to her that he was in charge, and she was more than thrilled.

But she longed to return the favor. Nadine had always been a generous lover, making sure that she gave at least as much as she received, and tonight was no exception. She wanted to please David. She wanted, also, to experience his body.

She reached for his zipper. He pulled her hand away immediately. She thought he was being playful, so she tried again. Again, he took her by the wrist and placed her hand back down on the bed beside her, only this time he held her there.

"Don't even think about it. Tonight, I'm pleasuring you," he said in a tone that rivaled the forcefulness of his kissing.

"Let me..."

"No." He was firm. "There will be time for me later. Tonight's about you."

"That's hardly fair," she said, trying to be coy.

"Oh, but it is. You see, there is nothing I want more than to explore your body and figure out what turns you on."

"You're doing a great job so far." She laughed nervously. Quietly.

"You're going to lie back and take it, Nadine. I don't want any argument. I'm going to explore every inch of you and all I want from you is indication as to whether you like it. In fact, from this moment on, all I want to hear from you is guidance—harder, faster, slower, softer. That sort of thing."

"Oh my."

"And don't you dare think that it's not fair. This has been my fantasy ever since I met you, and it's coming true."

"But what about you?"

"You mean my penis? I am aware of it. But I want to learn how to make you come before you ever meet my cock."

"Oh," Nadine managed. The words went to her clit and she felt lightheaded, as though all the blood had left her brain and she could no longer think. She didn't need to think, she reckoned. Not when Mr. Forceful was in charge. So she let him take the lead. It was what they both wanted.

"All right," she cooed as she reclined.

This was the most erotic encounter she had ever had. In the dim light of her warm room, nestled in scents of vanilla from the candle he'd stolen a moment away to light, she watched as David claimed his prize. He'd said he wanted to explore her and he did. His fingers glided over her belly to her jeans. He unbuttoned the top, unzipped her front and folded the triangles of denim down to reveal the white and pink lace panties she had on underneath. She was glad now that she had put in the time at the estheticians, even though a part of her had thought that they wouldn't go this far. She couldn't wait to get these jeans off and let him go exploring.

* * * *

"So, sex kitten," Marnie purred into the phone. "How did it go with the boy toy?"

"It was incredible," Nadine said. "And you can't call him that anymore."

"Oh, poo. You're no fun. Alfonso and I are meeting for a drink after work at *Fresco Forno*. You have to come. We're living vicariously through you, don't forget."

"All right. Can we sit on the heated patio?"

"Sure, why?"

"I'll bring Duchess."

"Who's Duchess?"

"My new best friend."

"What?"

"The furry kind. I got a dog."

"What?" Marnie yelled even louder this time.

"You can meet her later."

* * * *

When she got to *Fresco Forno*, Nadine walked through the cast iron gate and spotted her friends instantly. They waved and gesticulated. Alfonso was impossible to miss with his bright clothes and dark glasses.

"Hey, girl!" Alfonso said. Marnie lifted what appeared to be a Margarita.

"Isn't it a little late in the season for that?" I looked at the fancy cocktail glass with its wide brim and tall stem like an upside down sombrero on a pole.

"That's what heat lamps are for. Besides, they're on special, and I already ordered you one. Now who's this?"

Her friends looked at Duchess, who wagged her tail back at them.

"My new BFF, Duchess."

"BF, girl. You know dogs don't live forever. You're Puff, and Duchess is Little Jackie Paper."

"Oh hush," Nadine said. "She's here now and that's what matters."

Marnie said, "She's gorgeous." And Alfonso conceded.

"So, sit down, tie her to the table and spill it."

"All right, all right." Nadine fumbled with her bag, and put it on the ground. Duchess didn't need a leash. She understood the situation right away and curled up underneath the table.

"That's amazing," Marnie quipped. "She's so well trained."

"Her previous owner was a professional trainer. How lucky is that?"

"Was?"

"She's in a nursing home. They don't allow big dogs."

"How cruel."

"Yeah, I know," Nadine agreed. "I'll be taking Duchess to visit Mrs. Bronstein regularly. We're starting tomorrow evening, actually."

"Wow, that's really nice of you."

"Well… I should hope that if we were ever in Mrs. Bronstein's shoes, someone else would do the same."

"Okay, enough of this Pollyanna stuff. I've already filled Alfonso in as much as I could, but you have to give us the play by play. You were pretty cagey about it before."

"That's because," Nadine summoned her courage. She really loved her friends, but she was starting to fall in love with David. "I need you to not make fun. I think I really like him."

"Good Lord. Don't tell me you hear wedding bells already," Marnie said.

"I can just picture us all at your wedding," Alfonso began. "You could get married at Disneyland!"

They both cracked up but Nadine didn't find it amusing in the slightest.

"See?" she said. "That's what I'm talking about."

"Oh, honey, don't be offended. We're having our fun with you. What's the harm?"

It was pointless. Her friends were way more immature than they accused David of being. She stayed for drinks, but she kept the conversation focused on them instead of her.

* * * *

When Nadine rounded the bend to her street, she noticed from afar that there was a bouquet of flowers on her stoop. How thoughtful, she mused, that David would show his appreciation for their date that way. He was really quite something.

The orange and yellow gerberas were beautiful. How did David know they were her favorite? She brought them inside, took off her coat and hung it behind the door, tossed off her walking shoes and brought everything upstairs. She set the flowers down on her kitchen table, gave Duchess a fresh dish of water and only then did she finally think to open the card.

Nadine, I'm only in town for a week. I hope you'll have dinner with me. Yours, Allan.

Nadine almost fainted right on the spot in her own kitchen. She hadn't heard from Allan in nearly two years, since he'd moved. What had brought him back? And what, more importantly, had led him to believe that he could just drop off some flowers and suddenly she'd fall for his antics all over again. She stared at the card. His number was on the bottom, along with a 'PS' that read —

I know you haven't forgiven me, but I want to make it better. Please let me.

It was that confidence of his. That charm. She had missed him, in spite of every rational thought to the contrary. He knew how to talk to her, knew that she wanted to be told. But he had some nerve. How typical of him to breeze into town right after she had started something new. Nadine realized that she was happy for the first time in ages. Being out with David had made her alive again and she knew that he understood her.

She needed to see David. She shouldn't keep Allan's sudden appearance from him. It was too much to take in. They'd had an amazing night together, but if she told him about Allan and the depth of her history with him, she feared she'd reveal too much too soon, especially if she told him the whole truth—that Allan was the only guy she'd ever loved. Everyone, even her own parents, had believed Allan to be the guy for her, and she had too.

Why did he have to come back? And why now?

Nadine didn't want to make this seem like too much of a deal. She had to downplay the story. It was the only right thing to do. After all, she didn't know what Allan wanted. Maybe he was in town to announce his engagement to someone else. Maybe he was on business and wanted her to know he was sorry for breaking her heart so long ago. Whatever it was, she knew that she couldn't lie to David, but she also couldn't tell the whole truth.

She took Duchess for a walk to mull it over but found herself walking toward David's neighborhood. She hadn't seen his place, but surely it couldn't be as bad as he'd made it out to be. She was sure it wasn't a keg style frat house or anything. That just didn't seem to suit David.

If there was any good left in the world, she told herself, they'd run into each other by sheer kismet and she wouldn't have to call and instigate a conversation. There'd be something ominous about that. She wanted, instead, to say it casually. *Oh, by the way, this guy I used to know is in town and wants to meet up.*

After over an hour of walking, she had not seen him. Even Duchess was beginning to express that it was enough. She kept looking up at her with those soft brown eyes, so gentle a reminder of the night they first met, the date with David. Enough was enough. She summoned her courage and finally dialed David's number.

"Hey," he said, sounding pleased to hear from her.

"I'm in your neighborhood with Duchess. Wondering if you have time to see us."

"Oh, uh, sure. Where are you?"

"Out by Gold's Park."

"What are you doing there?"

"We just went for a run, that's all." She should have said walk, she realized. She wasn't dressed in running gear.

"Oh, okay."

"Can I come by?"

"Um, well, let me just ask the guys."

Nadine was surprised that he had to ask.

* * * *

David, however, wasn't asking so much as stalling, trying to figure out a way to avoid having Nadine come over. If she ever saw his place, he wanted at the very least to make sure that it was scoured and tidy. Tonight, it wasn't. But David couldn't lie. He wanted badly to tell her that his roommates had other things going on, but what possible reason could he give to not let her stop by? Plus, he wanted to see her.

"Sure, come over." He cringed as he gave her the exact address.

"That's very close. I'll be there in five."

"Great." David tried to sound enthusiastic and hospitable. "See you soon."

The second he got off the phone, he tore about the place like the Tasmanian Devil cartoon, only instead of wreaking havoc, he got rid of all the takeout containers on the coffee table, and shook out a blanket and laid it over the sofa to cover the stains.

He ran to his room and made his bed, but then he realized that he'd be better off concentrating on keeping her out of his room. He closed the door to the bedroom and sprang around, picking up Chris' socks that had been carelessly strewn about. Then he saw the mountain of dishes in the sink. There was no time to do them all, so—in his state of confusion and stress—he thought it'd look better if he hid the pile of dishes beneath a couple of tea towels. He draped the dishes like he'd draped the sofa then he looked down at himself. He was wearing sweatpants. He'd been studying. This would never do. He tore back into his room, found his jeans on the floor, shook them to get the balled up socks out of the legs. The doorbell rang. He tore off his sweatpants, put on the jeans, ripped off his old T-shirt and dug around for a nice one, but couldn't see one anywhere. The doorbell rang again. He checked the closet and nothing. The laundry hamper and...nothing. Where the heck was his nice shirt? He was tempted to put the old one back on but after a quick pit-sniff, he abandoned it. In the end, he came out of his room wearing his good jeans and his Star Wars sleeping shirt. Easily the most embarrassing moment of his life. Why hadn't she given him more time?

He got to the door by the third ring. Opening it, he saw a vision of beauty, fresh faced and with rosy cheeks.

"Nadine," he said, reaching out to her, wanting her in his arms again. He remembered the sounds he'd inspired in her the night before. She didn't motion to kiss him, but he kissed her cheek anyway.

Her tense posture told him that something was up. He hoped she didn't have regrets about what had happened between them. He was self-conscious about what he was wearing, wishing desperately that he was more put together.

"I was just taking a nap when you called," he told her, by way of explanation.

"And you sleep in Star Wars pajamas?" She giggled.

David looked down at his shirt and held it out. "This was a gift from my grandparents." Then he changed the topic. "Come on in."

"With Duchess, too?"

"Of course. Nobody's home right now."

"I thought you had to ask them about my visit earlier."

"Oh, right." David wanted to slap his head but there was nothing he could do. *Act cool*, he told himself, but it didn't seem to be working. He resigned himself to having been caught off guard, but he didn't let it affect his manners. He invited her into the messy fraternity style apartment and hoped that it didn't smell too much like socks or beer. She didn't seem to be too turned off, he reckoned, so the tour continued through the living room and into the kitchen. The doors to all the bedrooms were closed, which was very convenient. He hoped to keep her in the common space.

"Can I get you something to drink?" he asked. "Soda? Beer?"

"I guess you don't have any white wine."

"No," he said, again wishing that he'd been given the chance to prepare. Had he known that she was coming, he would have bought white wine. In fact, he should have bought it when they first started dating. This was a lesson learned.

Nadine gave a reassuring smile. "Okay, I'll have a beer."

"Really?"

"Sure."

"Cool. Have a seat." David gestured at the couch that was covered with a crocheted blanket that one of his roommates' grandmothers had made in the 1980s.

Nadine sat down carefully. She had not been in a place like this in a long time, though she'd been no stranger to this type of home when she was at university. She'd just outgrown it, she thought, which led her to wonder whether she could ever feel comfortable with this. Could she have a boyfriend who was fine with using milk crates for bookshelves? She looked around. There were posters on the wall — not utterly tasteless — there was Einstein on the south wall and some fractals behind the television. But this was not a home, not really. This was more of a dwelling. It didn't seem to reflect David. How could it? He was just one of three here.

She examined the DVDs beneath the old television set — alien movies and sci-fi thrillers. There were also cinematic classics — *A Clockwork Orange*, *2001: A Space Odyssey*, and, weirdly, *Valley of the Dolls*. Boy movies, mostly. Smart boy movies, she reckoned, but nonetheless boy movies. She sighed. She was dating a boy. Well, not 'dating', exactly. They'd been on one date, she found herself observing.

Her mind followed the thought further... One sexy date. She'd had the best sexual experience of her life so far with a guy who draped his furniture. She sighed. *Why is the world so confusing and unfair?*

When David returned from the kitchen with two cans of beer — *Does he not even own glasses?* — Nadine tried to see him for the man he had been the night before, but all she could see was the boy who stood in front of her.

"Cheers," he said, passing her a can.

She was going to make the best of it. "Cheers."

Perhaps Alfonso and Marnie had not been so wrong after all. And there really was nothing wrong with two consenting adults having a sexual tryst. It didn't have to be more than that. And, really, what did it matter if he always came over to her place? She was the one with Egyptian cotton sheets. She was the one with matching furniture and glasses. Area rugs. *You get to a certain point, and you want area rugs.*

She took a sip of her cheap beer and knew that she'd better start talking, because she'd be tipsy by the end of this can and it was almost certain to lead to a headache.

"So, uh, David. Can I tell you something?"

"Of course."

"Well, when I came home tonight, there was a message on my doorstep. It seems an old friend is in town and wants to get together."

David nodded. Nadine knew that she'd copped out. Rehearsing the lines on the way over had not helped. She continued, "Actually, he's my old boyfriend, from a long time ago. He's here for a week and he wants to have dinner."

"The fiancé who left?" David asked.

Nadine nodded. She'd forgotten that she'd told him about that. Relief came over her. At least now there was a chance that he'd understand how important this was.

"Cool," David said.

Nadine was startled. "Okay, so you're cool with it. I just wanted to check."

"Why wouldn't I be?"

"I don't know. Some guys..." She couldn't finish the sentence. What had she expected him to say? What had she wanted? Why was she somehow disappointed?

"Do I have any reason to stress out about it?" David asked.

"Well, no."

"So, then, no problem."

Nadine paused. Of course he would jump to that conclusion. Her words had guided him there. She had still not been entirely honest. It was now or never and Nadine knew that in order to live with herself, she had to be forthright.

"Here's the thing," she said.

"Oh, there's a thing."

She smiled as if to lighten the load. "When he left, I was devastated and broken-hearted, and I haven't seen him since and now he's back."

"For a week."

"Yeah, for a week."

"When did you two break up?"

"It's been about... Let's see..." She counted on her fingers. "It has been nearly two years."

"That's a long time. How long were you together?"

"Eight years." She looked down at her can. She couldn't look at David. She felt like she'd burst into tears if she did. This was all so emotional and so strange. Allan had been a ghost who haunted her dreams at night and to think that he'd decided to come back now. He'd always had terrible timing. "We were high-school sweethearts."

"I see. And he left suddenly?"

"At our engagement party, actually."

"Oh." David made a face. It was clear that he was unimpressed.

"Yeah, which I guess is better than being left at the altar, but it was still the most painful experience of my life. All those guests. All those eyes watching."

"Did he make some sort of public announcement or something?"

"No, he left quietly. He told me it was over and that he'd already packed his bags. He said he was leaving and not coming back and that he was sorry. But, of course, he didn't consider the fact that my parents had a whole garden full of friends and relatives waiting to shower us with affection."

As she relived the memory of still having to offer everyone cake and small talk, Nadine's tears flowed freely. She couldn't hold them back. "It was awful."

"Nadine, I'm sorry." He wiped her tears away with his thumb. "It sounds like he's an ass. Is this the first time you've heard from him since?"

"No, he called a couple of weeks later from New York. He said he needed time to figure some stuff out, that he wasn't ready to be married. He told me not to wait for him."

She took another sip of her beer and looked around her. Suddenly she felt silly. "I'm sorry I'm telling you all this and we barely even know each other. I just didn't want to make you jealous."

"I'm not the jealous type," David said.

It wasn't the response she'd hoped for, though she didn't exactly know what she'd wanted. Why had she wanted so badly to tell him?

"Okay."

"Well, I mean, unless you want me to be jealous."

She rolled her eyes. How immature. "David, of course I don't *want* you to be jealous."

"But this is what you came to tell me about, isn't it? This is why you came over."

"Well, yeah. I thought you should know."

"So you're planning on having dinner with this guy who was a total asshole to you a few years ago and you want me to know so that I won't be jealous." David's tone was cold and judicial, like he was a scholar summarizing an argument.

Nadine nodded. "Well, it sounds really stupid when you put it like that."

"Like what?" David still had the air of a debater composing a brilliant rebuttal in his mind.

"I don't know. I'm not sure why I told you."

"To absolve yourself of any guilt you might have?" David's words sounded harsh and accusing.

"Maybe."

"Just tell me this. Are you planning on getting back together with him?"

"No."

"Are you still in love with him?"

Nadine was silent for a second too long. "No," she said quietly. But it was too weak a response. She needed to elaborate. "I want to see him. I never got closure. And it is complicated. I mean, our families still send Christmas cards. Everyone thought we'd be together. Everyone thought he was the one."

"Did you?"

"Of course. I was going to marry him."

"If your goal was to come over here to reassure me, you're not doing a very good job. Why don't you just have dinner with him first before you tell me about feelings you might hypothetically have. Two years is a long time. I'm sure you've both changed. Besides, there's a reason people break up with one another. That's my belief. The whole on-again-off-again is for chick flicks. In real life, when it's over, it's over. People move on."

Nadine thought of the bouquet and wondered if what David was saying was true. Had Allan moved on? Probably. He was probably just trying to make up for the harm he'd caused. She'd find out soon enough.

"You're right," she said. "I just wanted you to know."

"I appreciate you telling me, but you don't have to get nervous that I'm going to get jealous. I hate playing games."

"I wasn't playing a game with you."

"I'm glad you told me." He leaned in to kiss her but Nadine wasn't too sure anymore. They shared the most chaste kiss they'd ever had. Then Nadine sipped her beer and changed the subject. She asked about one of the DVDs and David proceeded to tell her about the alien plan to attack Earth and the cyborg-human alliance that saved the planet.

Chapter Fifteen

When she left, they kissed again, this time a little more romantically, though it was hard to achieve romance with beer breath. She mulled the encounter over in her head as she walked home with Duchess at her side. He'd seemed standoffish to her. She'd dated jealous guys in the past — Allan was the worst — and maybe she was more used to that sort of behavior. To her, it seemed like David didn't really care. She reasoned that they'd only been on one date, but as she went over the situation from all angles, she considered that if the roles had been reversed, she'd have felt very threatened. Was he simply more confident than she was or had he not invested in their connection yet? No doubt her friends would tell her that he was young and playing the field, but it hadn't felt that way to her on their date.

The more she thought about the encounter at David's place, the more displeased she became with herself. Why had she needed to tell him? A different kind of woman would have kept it to herself, gone out with

Allan for dinner *then* told… If there was anything to tell.

As she and Duchess walked through the neighborhood streets, she looked at all the pretty houses and wondered if she would ever find The One. She wasn't too sure about David. His apartment scared her. There, he seemed like someone who could host a good kegger—not at all like the guy she was out with the other night. And what was with the Star Wars pajamas? Was that what he lounged around in by himself? If she went out with him, she was probably destined to wait for at least a decade before he wanted some of the stuff she wanted, she thought as she watched a random couple pull up to their house, and get out of their car. The woman carried groceries. The man had a big box from an electronics shop. They were probably going to make dinner and set up new speakers or something like that. Something cozy.

At home, she felt restless. The bouquet mocked her, dared her to call Allan. She wanted to ignore it. She didn't want to give him the satisfaction of having this kind of emotional grip on her. *Who does he think he is?*

She wondered if her parents knew he was in town. It occurred to her that she might want to call them first. If nothing else, it'd be a way to procrastinate. She really wanted to delay the inevitable, at least until the beer wore off. She dialed her parents.

"Nadine, what a surprise," her dad said. "We're just sitting here with the Jordans having a glass of red. Why don't you come on over? There's someone here who wants to say hello."

She could tell that the Jordans were all listening in on the conversation. Her dad was making quite the display of it.

"Um, is it Allan?"

"It is. You must have gotten the flowers."

"Yeah."

"Why don't you come on by? We'll give you two space if you need to talk."

This was so abrupt. She didn't want to go over there now, didn't want to have yet another public showdown with Allan, even if this was a different form. A reunion was different from a parting, but still. Why did everything have to be so public with him? Sure, it was family, but there would still be four more people than just the two of them.

"Uh, okay."

There was no point in delaying, though. She'd be forced to see him one way or another. At least if the family was there, she reasoned, she wouldn't punch him in the face or tell him how horrible it had been after he left. And she wouldn't reference David, since her family didn't even know about him yet. And if everything went absolutely horrendously wrong, her mom would be there to hold her, feed her and give her wine.

"Great. See you soon," her dad said.

* * * *

Nadine observed that her parents kept the yard immaculate as she pulled into the driveway. For a second she felt that she'd been cursed to have parents with such a great marriage and an all-round Norman Rockwell type of family. It made finding her match a real challenge. Maybe the reason she was so picky was that she secretly feared that no man lived up to her expectations. Allan had seemed to, but that was a long time ago.

As she parked, she felt her shoulders tense up. That was where she carried her stress, and she was definitely feeling anxious. So many months had passed. She took a moment to look in the rearview mirror. Her lipstick. Where was it? She scoured her bag looking for it. Duchess panted. She clearly wanted out. Nadine's throat felt dry, like she wasn't sure she'd be able to talk. She felt short of breath.

Just then, before she'd had a chance to find her lipstick, the front door opened and Allan emerged. He looked the same. His broad shoulders and dark features still stunned her. He was a very handsome man. It wasn't just his height, but the way he carried himself, so assured and smooth. She flung open the door and got out—now or never.

"Hey." He opened his arms to her. She entered his embrace cautiously at first, but once she was in his arms, it felt so familiar to be there. His scent was still the same. His strong grasp still felt as good as it used to. He squeezed her tight. "It's so good to see you," he said.

"You too." To her own surprise, she meant it. Up until that moment, the encounter had seemed a burden, but now that she was in his arms, it felt right that he should call on her. She wouldn't have wanted it any other way. The past had passed. And here they were in the present. She found herself immediately curious about what he'd been up to.

"Who's this?" He gestured at Duchess, who had not jumped out through the front seat the way some dogs would have. She sat in the back, wagging her tail.

Nadine opened the door for her. "This is Duchess."

The Setter jumped out and Allan put his hand out to acquaint himself. "Wow, she's a real beauty. When did you get her?"

"Just yesterday, as a matter of fact."

"Whoa."

"Yeah. Exciting times," she said.

"I'll say." He looked at her as though he was trying to figure out what it meant that she'd become a dog owner, but he didn't ask about it. Instead he said, "You look great, Nadine. Better than ever."

"Thanks," she said. "You too." But she didn't want to dwell on appearance. It was awkward. "So how's New York treating you?"

"Good," he replied, nodding. "Actually, I should say great. I've been promoted twice this past year and I've just put a down payment on a sweet condo. It's got two bedrooms and a great view of Central Park."

Same old Allan. Cool as ever.

"Wow," she said. "Congratulations. Your parents must be so proud."

"Yeah, they're inside. They're excited about seeing you."

Nadine nodded.

"I am too. I was really looking forward to seeing you, Nadine. And now I know exactly why."

"Okay, why?"

"Something's been missing ever since we split up. I haven't felt right about it, the way I treated you. I want you to know I'm really sorry."

"It's in the past now, Allan. Let's not hash it up. At least not right here, right now. I'd rather just hang out with your parents."

"You got it. But will you let me take you out to dinner?"

"Sure," she said, a little too quickly.

"Good. There's some stuff I'd like to discuss and anyway, I have something for you that I should have given you a long time ago."

"Really?"

"Yeah. It's not from me, but it's really important."

"That is very mysterious, Allan."

"I know. I don't mean to be. Let's just say there's a surprise coming your way."

"Well, you're full of surprises."

Allan looked momentarily hurt and defensive, but then he said, "I'm just gonna let that go. I deserve whatever you dish out."

"Let's go in." Nadine locked her car doors and the three of them walked in through the house single file, with Duchess in the back.

The Jordans were in the sun room, the glass-covered back patio that Nadine's parents used year-round to entertain guests. Michigan was not exactly a warm climate, but the enclosed space meant that any time it was sunny, it felt warm on the indoor patio.

Everyone got up out of their chairs to greet Nadine, but the attention went straight to her new best friend.

Her mother spoke first. "Who's this?"

"Everyone, this is Duchess. She's part of my life now. I got her yesterday from the SPCA." Nadine elaborated about Mrs. Bronstein and Duke, but she left David out of the story. She was aware of it, but she could analyze herself later. It was very odd to come face to face with her past like this. The Jordans hugged her and carried on as though they still considered her a soon-to-be daughter-in-law.

Nadine's dad gave her the update to the impromptu plans. "We invited Todd and Samantha over, too. They're coming for dinner. We thought we'd order in."

"Oh, okay," Nadine said. Her brother and sister-in-law were coming, too? What was this? Some kind of awkward family reunion? "I'll probably need to leave early, as I have some business to attend to."

"On a Sunday?" Jeraldine Jordan asked. The Jordans were strict Christians in the sense that they observed Sunday as a day of rest, and apparently also as a day of paying unplanned visits.

"I've been making a go of my business in addition to my job," Nadine explained. "Which means I'm busy all the time now." She laughed nervously.

Jeraldine Jordan was a homemaker and not particularly amused. "Don't tell me you're back at the investment firm and now running a business on the side, dear. My goodness." She had a way of sounding concerned, but Nadine detected a touch of insecurity in the observation.

"After the firm let me go, I went back to my old job at the bookstore at UMich. It gives me health benefits and it's steady and easy, and I can even bring Duchess to work with me, so it affords me the chance to launch my dream."

Mr. Jordan enquired, "And what's this business of yours?"

"Well, remember Grandpa Winston? I'm following in his footsteps. Restoring furniture."

The Jordans looked at each other like they were totally puzzled by Nadine's words. There was a pause as they took it in. Finally, Jeraldine asked the question that Nadine was sure they were all thinking. "But how can you do that? Isn't there a lot of heavy lifting involved?"

"There is some," Nadine conceded. "And sometimes I get help, but most of the work is sanding, staining and that sort of thing."

Their doubtful expressions hurt Nadine's feelings more than she let on. "Anyway, it's going well. I've made a great deal of sales this month and now I need to deliver on my promises and that's why I'll have to bow out a little early tonight." She felt that the words sounded harsh, so she added a polite, "I'm sorry."

"Allan came all the way from New York," Nadine's mom said.

"Yeah," Nadine countered. "And if I'd known he was coming I could have moved things around in my schedule, but as it is, I have to put a final coat of varnish on a bookshelf tonight and I have to try to get to bed in time to wake up for Monday morning."

"Who'd like another glass of merlot?" her mother asked no one in particular. "Nadine? Would you come and help me?"

"Sure."

Nadine followed her mother into the kitchen. As soon as they were behind closed doors, her mother turned and faced her with an expression of so much urgency that Nadine remembered what it was like to be a child about to get in trouble.

"Allan's still in love with you. You might want to see if you can fit that into your schedule."

"Did he say anything?"

"He doesn't have to. Look at him."

"Mom, quit being dramatic. He broke up with me a long time ago. Remember?"

"Maybe so, but he came back for you."

"You don't know that. His parents live in Ann Arbor, too, you know."

"Oh, please. They go see him every chance they get. They love going to Broadway and the museums and all that jazz."

"You're jumping to conclusions, and you know it."

"He's a good guy, Nadine. An excellent catch."

"He left me. Did you forget?"

"We were all young once, dear."

"It wasn't even two years ago."

"He's matured a lot since then."

"Why are you being like this? What if I don't want to get married anymore?"

"Don't you?"

Nadine shook her head. She hadn't been forced into acknowledging this to her mother before and so she'd kept it to herself, figuring that one day her mother would simply notice that instead of a husband, there was a different kind of lifestyle, a family made up of friends, a thriving business, Duchess and maybe a hot young lover.

"I dodged a bullet, Mom. I really did. That's how I feel."

"Well, it won't hurt you to at least be nice to him while he's here."

"I'm being nice," she blurted in a tone that was less than sweet. "I'm letting him take me out for dinner."

Her mother scoffed.

"What?" Nadine quipped. "He broke my heart and left. What do I owe him? I think I'm being plenty nice by even being here right now."

"Nadine," her mother said softly. This was the way she got what she wanted. She had this perfect ability to be gentle. "You're still hurting. I understand. Hear him out. Let him apologize. It's obvious he wants to." Nadine felt that her mother's embrace was enough to make her put her proverbial sword and shield down. After all, they all wanted the best for her, didn't they? Even the Jordans. It was not their fault that Allan had bolted. And it was true what she had admitted to her mother. She did feel that his leaving had been a blessing. It had taken some time to reach that conclusion, but she knew that if they had gotten married when they'd planned to, she wouldn't have been ready. She had needed to grow.

When Nadine and her mother re-emerged, the Jordans were in the middle of their story about their last trip to New York City. Specifically, they were telling the story of seeing *Phantom of the Opera*. Nadine couldn't help but notice that they still spoke over the top of each other, like they always had.

When Mr. Jordan said, "So we're already late when we leave the hotel and..." then Mrs. Jordan jumped in with, "Getting a cab is a nightmare. Don't let anybody tell you otherwise." Mr. Jordan continued, "Finally a guy picks us up but then we get stuck in traffic..." Mrs. Jordan interjected, "There's a parade." Mr. Jordan took over the story-telling, "So I'm watching the clock and the meter..." But Mrs. Jordan wasn't going to let him hog the spotlight so she added, "And the driver tells us he's going to take another route."

Allan's parents were great, Nadine observed, but their stories were always co-creations that meandered and made little sense. She sipped her merlot and looked at Allan, sitting idly by while his parents talked. How strange this was, for the two of them to be here — in the same room together for the first time since the most awful day of her life — and there was no acknowledgment of that awkwardness. Instead, there was a mundane beginning of a story that seemed to go nowhere and wasn't at all entertaining.

Mr. Jordan finally got to the point about how they had got there just in time to brush elbows with Amy Sedaris and Stephen Colbert. Mr. Jordan reiterated a funny moment they'd all shared. It wasn't really a laugh-out-loud moment, but Nadine chuckled anyway. It felt good to defuse the situation, because in her own mind, she was going over all the questions she had for Allan.

The doorbell rang and her father shifted to get up, but Allan gestured to him to stay.

"Don't worry, I'll get it," Allan said, taking charge. "It can only be Todd and Samantha."

Nadine shook her head at Allan as she watched him go for the door. Why not just call her father Dad like he used to? He sure was making himself at home. And the crazy part was, her dad clearly loved every second of it. She watched his face as he sat there on the couch, anticipating Allan's next move. Everyone fell silent in the indoor patio space.

Then there was an uproar when Allan opened the door. Hugs and hoots came thundering through the halls.

"Look at you. You haven't changed a bit," Todd said.

Allan countered with, "Good to see you, man," and a firm slap on the back. To Samantha, he was chivalrous and gave her a hug and told her how much he'd missed her.

Nadine looked around. She seemed to be the only one who was not beside herself with glee that Allan had come back. The others either had amnesia or assumed that she had forgiven Allan completely.

Dinner was long. Her mother and Jeraldine Jordan gave Thanksgiving recipes and canning tips to her and Samantha, while her father, Frank Jordan and Todd talked about work and getting out to their cabins to do repairs and go fishing. Nadine felt that this was a tiny taste of what life could have been like had they been four married couples. She was grateful that, on occasion, she could look around the table for a reassuring glance from Allan.

After dinner and coffee, Nadine announced that she had to go.

"Let me walk you out." Allan stood up. The whole evening had been going in this direction so Nadine thought it ludicrous to refuse now. After a night of public courtesy, the least he could do was give her a few minutes of alone time.

"Thank you," she said. "Thanks, everybody, for a nice dinner. It was a great surprise."

"Don't work too hard," Mr. Jordan said. And everyone at the table laughed.

"All right," Nadine said. There was nothing else she felt she could say.

She and Allan looked at each other and headed for the hallway. He helped her with her jacket, as he always had. She'd give him that much. He was gallant. He held the door for her and she walked out of her parents' home feeling confused, yet loved in a strangely familiar way. Duchess followed.

"It was nice to see your parents," she said.

"They love you, you know," he assured her. "Sorry they gave you a hard time about the furniture stuff. You know they're traditional."

"I know." She nodded. She opened the back door and Duchess jumped in.

"But don't be fooled. I bet they're in there right now talking about what an incredible girl you are. When they're in New York, they talk of nothing else," he divulged. And as though he had not made his point, he added, "Believe me."

She nodded again. "Well, I've always liked them."

"It's been a treat to see your parents as well. You should all come and visit."

Nadine's face betrayed the bewilderment within. So much had gone unsaid at this point that it felt utterly strange to imagine that she and her parents would ever take a trip together to visit Allan. She unlocked the car door. The silence must have given Allan a moment to consider the odd nature of his invitation.

"Is anything the matter?" he asked.

"Well, Allan, I think it's remarkable that you feel like you can come back, not give anything at all by way of explanation and think we can simply pick up right where we left off."

"I am expecting to explain and properly apologize when we meet for dinner." He held onto the door as Nadine got in. "Believe me, I know I was awful and I'm not assuming we can pick up where we left off."

"Good."

"Because I know I hurt you."

"You did, Allan. It's true. But that's not all. I mean, how can you assume I'm going to drop everything and run into your arms? You don't know how busy I am with work. You never even asked if I'm seeing anyone. It's just a whole lot of assuming."

"Well, are you?"

"We can talk at dinner. I really have to get to work. Besides, you should get back to the dinner party."

"All right, so Tuesday evening?"

Nadine rolled down the window so that she could shut the car door without slamming it on him. Like a gentleman, he picked up on the cues and closed the door.

"Yes, Tuesday," she said. "What time?"

"I'll pick you up at seven."

"Okay."

He reached through the open window and took her left hand off the steering wheel. Holding onto it, he guided her arm gently out of the window and brought her hand up to his mouth. He bent down and kissed the back of her hand.

"I'm looking forward to it," he said.

She nodded. "Me too."

* * * *

Alone in her garage later, she played Mozart. It was the only music she could stand to listen to. Allan could be so arrogant and presumptuous, she told herself as she applied the final layer of varnish to the side table, making it slick and smooth the way she imagined the world saw Allan.

If only it was clear. If only she could have said, 'In fact, I am dating someone special. His name is David and he is everything you're not.'

But she was unable to do this because she was entirely uncertain about David. In the harsh light of day, after the pheromones and lust had worn off, she'd seen a side that she didn't know about. She couldn't date someone so young and messy. She couldn't understand his youthful and cavalier ways. It was as though the guy she had gone to see was a totally different guy from the one who'd taken her on a date.

How can I be so clueless about men?

Chapter Sixteen

The next day, Nadine took Duchess for a long walk through the city. She wanted to clear her head and get some perspective, but she ended up just walking around enjoying the surroundings. Though she'd lived in Ann Arbor all her life, she didn't spend nearly enough time admiring the old buildings. This was an incredibly rich place in terms of architecture, she mused. As she turned back onto West Liberty Street, she saw her Grandpa's old shop. It was such a beautiful brick building that housed what was once Grandpa Winston's pride and joy. She felt a tremendous amount of pain in her heart. How she missed him and the years she had spent with him there. She'd learned everything from him. As she looked around, she realized that the neighborhood had barely changed. Mrs. Barlow's music supply shop was still next door. There was still a Laundromat and a bakery exactly where they had been. Only the big wooden sign that had once said 'Winston's Fine Furniture' was gone. Otherwise, the place looked the same. She hadn't gone in since her parents had sold it off. She didn't even know the new owner and had never thought she'd introduce herself. As she approached, a notice in the window caught her eye. On further inspection, it was a small poster with some interior photos. It said 'For lease'.

It couldn't be. She looked closer, double checked the address on the poster to see if it matched the one she was standing in front of. Sure enough, her grandfather's store was available. This was something she had not anticipated, nor had she expected to have so strong a physical reaction. Her hands went clammy. Her pulse raced. It felt as though she'd been drawn to see this. The sign itself had beckoned her.

Just then Mrs. Barlow emerged from her shop.

"Nadine?" Her voice was warm and instantly recognizable.

"Mrs. Barlow!" She ran to her and hugged her.

"Why, I haven't see you since…" Her words trailed off.

"I know, after everything, I just… Well, I couldn't come back."

"I understand. We all miss your grandfather. We still talk about him a lot, you know. It's like his spirit never left the neighborhood. Anyway, how've you been? Are you still at the investment firm?"

"No, I left that. I realized I wanted to work in the furniture business."

"You what?" Mrs. Barlow covered her mouth in surprise, and it looked for a second as though she fought back tears.

Nadine nodded. "Yeah, I've been working out of my garage. I took my old job at the bookstore back so I'd have health insurance and a steady paycheck, but I've been doing better and better with restoration."

"It's in your blood."

"Grandpa did teach me everything he knew."

"You were the apple of his eye, you know. Don't get me wrong. He loved your dad, mom and Todd too, but he talked about you nonstop around here. He was so proud of you. He'd be so proud to know you're in the business."

At that, Nadine burst into tears. It was too much to take in. She missed him so much.

"Is the shop space really up for lease?"

"It is."

"I can't believe it."

"Well, the new owner, Jack Harrington, didn't have your grandfather's skill or business sense, you know. He couldn't make a go of it. Gave it an honest try. It's been... What? Nearly two years now. He ran through his savings. You can't blame him for throwing in the towel."

She shook her head. No, she couldn't blame him.

"I wonder how much he's asking."

"I don't know, there's a new building owner, a really good-looking young guy. Are you single? He'd be perfect for you."

"It's complicated," Nadine said, not wanting to get into it. "I wonder if the shop still has that tiny apartment upstairs. Did you ever see it?"

"Sure, it was a neat layout, but I know for a fact that Jack doesn't live there. You sure you're not seeing anyone? He's very cute."

"Mrs. Barlow!" Nadine blushed. "Stop."

"What? You can't blame me for asking. The only kind of love affairs I get to follow are the ones I live through vicariously."

"Well, if you must know, I've got too much man-drama right now as it is. I really just want to clear my head of men and focus on getting my business up and running."

"Sure, dear." Mrs. Barlow looked up into the dark depths of the upstairs windows of the heritage building. "Do you remember when you were just a little girl and you used to stay up there with George?"

"Of course," she said, recalling the scent of cinnamon tea and brilliantine and her grandfather's woolen blankets and Buddy all combined to create that familiar smell of home. "The view from up there was wonderful. All that afternoon sun."

"Yes. I think Jack just uses it for storage."

"Strange. It was such an inviting place to live."

Mrs. Barlow nodded. "Well, I don't mean to be forward, but maybe you should have a look."

"You know what? I will." She looked around, as though she couldn't quite take it all in. "It can't hurt to look, right?"

Mrs. Barlow gave her a pat on the back. She was such a kind and gentle woman. Nadine felt terrible for not having visited. It seemed silly now that she was here, but it had pained her to think of seeing this neighborhood without Grandpa Winston being in it anymore.

She went inside the shop. It had the same smell of wooden floors and she saw dust and beeswax furniture polish.

"Can I help you?" The shopkeeper popped his head up from behind the counter where he had been reading the newspaper and drinking tea.

"Are you Jack?"

"I am."

"I saw the sign out front."

He offered a handshake.

* * * *

After work, Nadine needed to strip paint off a dresser in the tiny little window between her paid job and the date she had agreed to. Two hours was about one-third of the time it normally took, but she was on a deadline, and she was ready to work fast.

She scurried home, not stopping for a bite to eat, and jumped into her coveralls. Thankfully, she had taken Duchess for a long walk at lunch, she mused, because there was not enough time for another one. Yet, her sweet companion came with her into the workspace and took her spot on the warm dog bed that protected her from the concrete floor.

With precision of focus and incredible superhuman speed, Nadine set to work applying the chemicals she needed to use to dissolve paint that had been on the piece since before the Second World War. Old-fashioned oil paint was the toughest, but she had the solution. Layers upon layers began to peel off and she took her scraper to the surface and helped the process along, stripping the piece right down to the wood on only the first application in some areas. Other areas took more work. Two and a half hours passed with Nadine completely unaware of time. She was in the zone. This was the only way she ever got to such a meditative state. Working with furniture made her feel like she was fulfilling her life's purpose. All her cares and troubles melted away and all that mattered was seeing this object emerge, as fresh as it had been when it was first built. She loved to think about that, how all of the pieces she worked with came from a time when people actually built. In those days, people didn't go to Ikea and buy lacquered particleboard to assemble themselves. Carpenters worked on a project from start to finish. She imagined that if she were alive back then, she would have been a carpenter.

The buzzer on her cell phone signaled that it was time to move on, and it was probably for the best as she was getting cold working in the open garage with a fan set to send the toxic fumes away. In spite of gloves, her mask and coveralls, she felt the chill and looked forward to her warm shower.

Nadine washed her hands with the industrial strength orange exfoliating soap she kept by the downstairs sink. She dried them on her coveralls and went upstairs, eager to escape the fumes that would linger in the garage for hours, even with the carport open and the fan on. How desperately she wanted a work space.

She took off her coveralls and hung them on the banister and continued upstairs straight to the bathroom to take a shower. There wasn't much time. She had promised to be ready by seven. She took her clothes off quickly and placed them neatly on the counter. When she looked at herself in the mirror, she hardly recognized her body. All the physical labor she had been doing lately had changed her. The tummy she had spent her early twenties being self-conscious of was gone and her arms were muscular. Her phone signaled that she had a text message, so she looked for it in the heap of clothes. It was Allan.

Hey, princess. I'm leaving now. Can't wait to see you.

She did a double take. It had been a long time since anyone had called her princess, and the name no longer fit. She'd outgrown it long ago and it occurred to her in that moment that the girl Allan had asked out, the girl he had been so eager to see, no longer existed.

This date didn't seem at all like the act of kindness her mother had convinced her it could be. It seemed like a huge mistake.

* * * *

True to his word, Allan arrived at seven. He was exactly on time. She was running late. Though she was still wrapped in a towel, she flew down the stairs and opened the door.

"Come on up," she said. "I'm almost ready."

As they reached the top of the stairs, she offered him a glass of wine and told him that she just had to put on the finishing touches.

"The reservation's for seven," he said.

"It's seven now."

"Yeah, so we should probably head right there."

"But, you know me. You know I'm always running a little behind, and we still have to drive there. Why didn't you make the reservation for seven-thirty?"

"I thought you said we shouldn't make assumptions anymore."

"I did, but..." Her words trailed off. "Never mind. I'll be ready in a minute."

It wasn't true. Fifteen minutes had passed before she emerged from the bathroom, wearing her favorite BCBG tight blue dress that she'd had no use for this past year. Tonight was the night. But she had started to perspire because of the tight deadline so she'd been slowed down because she'd needed to apply more deodorant and take a tissue to her forehead where there was some beading.

"You look gorgeous."

"Thanks," she said. "Let's go. We're late."

"I called Pacific Rim and pushed back our reservation. Don't worry."

Nadine sighed a breath of relief. "Why didn't you tell me? I was rushing."

"I do want to eat some time before ten," he joked. "I know you can spend forever on your hair."

Nadine didn't laugh.

When they arrived, Allan took charge, holding all the doors for her and taking her coat for the coat check. She remembered what it was like to be his girlfriend. She wanted to resist his chivalrous gestures, but she figured that she might as well enjoy them. Besides, her mother would ask her about all of the details later, so she sat back and let Allan be Allan.

He examined the wine list as though it was in a language that only he understood. When the sommelier came, they conversed about regions and bouquets and all kinds of things that Nadine didn't know much about. Allan selected a bottle of wine that earned a nod of approval from the discerning expert who promptly returned, uncorked and poured a tiny amount into Allan's glass for him to judge. It suited him perfectly, Nadine noticed, to be treated this way. It had been a while since she'd spent any significant amount of time with Allan and she noticed that he had refined some of his mannerisms. He'd become ever more the gentleman he used to be. He was much more visually successful than he used to be. It was all in the details. His luxurious BMW, the silver Rolex watch that suited his wrist, the complex aroma of his cologne, his pressed shirt, the perfectly tailored jacket. Allan had become more of himself, that much was obvious. And she couldn't help but admit that it was nice to see. She still let him occupy a very significant place in her heart. All of her formative years had included him. Besides, it felt nice to be out with such a dignified and powerful man. It was an unusual treat.

They sipped their wine and Nadine relaxed into this date.

"So, as I was saying Sunday, there've been a lot of changes. You'd love the property I bought. I want you to see it. The balcony would suit you just perfectly."

Nadine found herself strangely sucked into his world. It was nearly impossible to be around Allan and not be allured by his magnetism. He exuded confidence and security and he was sexier than ever. It wasn't just her. Anyone would fall prey to those dark eyes and that infectious smile. It was also in the generally pleasant demeanor he showed the world. He knew exactly how to talk to the servers and everyone around them. She'd always admired the effortlessness with which he carried himself, like he knew that others received a great deal of pleasure from interacting with him.

When Allan ordered, the server made a point of complimenting his taste.

In spite of her best attempts to repress all of the passionate memories they shared, Nadine found herself falling for Allan's charm.

After the food had arrived, she blamed the coconut curry soup. Her senses were overwhelmed. Some blame also had to go to the peppercorn and wasabi seared Kobe steak. She'd give Allan that, too. The man knew food. He was definitely traditional, but he knew how to show a lady a good time.

"Nadine, I want you to know I've done a lot of growing over the past couple of years. I'm not the same person, I swear." He put down his fork and knife.

"You seem like you've become more of yourself," Nadine said, though she didn't know whether it was a compliment or an insult.

"I've learned a lot. I know I hurt you. It's the biggest regret of my life." He looked down at his dinner but didn't touch it. "To think that I had you and gave you up. It tears me up inside."

"You've had other girlfriends since?"

"Of course," he said without hesitation. "Lots."

Nadine nodded, feeling a combination of relief and nausea at the thought. It figured that a guy like him would have had a lot of girlfriends. It had been one of her biggest insecurities during their relationship. She'd obsessed over the amount of girls who had crushes on him and feared that his curiosity would tear them apart.

"But none of them ever compared to you."

This comment, spoken so sincerely, couldn't fail to arouse some form of sentimentality and nostalgia in Nadine. She'd longed to hear him say this and had fantasized about these very words for a long time.

She wanted more. "Go on."

"We had it all, Nadine. Our history together, our great sexual connection, the fact that our families already love each other. I wanted you to be the mother of my kids."

"But you left" — Nadine sat back in her chair, more solemn than before — "in an abrupt and downright cruel way."

"I felt like I had no other choice."

"You could have at least waited until after the party. Or hell, you could have figured it out before. You left me with a houseful of guests who wanted an explanation. Do you have any idea how mortifying that was for me?"

He leaned in, and looked like he was in pain just thinking about it. "I'm sorry. I would never do that now. I've changed."

"That's hard for me to believe. I mean, you come back with this flair of arrogance and call me up and expect that I've been waiting for you."

"You're not married."

She was aghast. "No, I'm not."

"Then it isn't a lost cause. I don't care if there's a boyfriend. I can win out in the end. We're soulmates. I know it."

"Allan, this isn't a game. You don't have to beat someone in a wrestling match."

"But I will if you want me to. Anything. You name it."

"I'd never ask you to compete for me."

"So there is someone to compete with?"

Nadine nodded. "There is."

"What's his name?"

"I'm not telling you." She knew very well how Allan could get. If he still had the temper he used to, he might just fly out of here and go cause a scene. That was his specialty. It had appealed to her when she was younger and he had in fact roughed up other guys in the name of love. And for some primal and irrational reason, she still found it hot. It was impossible to explain.

"Then tell me what he's got that I don't have."

"It's not a competition."

"Level with me, Nadine. I mean, I know you. I know you wanted us to get married and I know that even though you're putting up a brave front here, you did wait for me, at least for a while. Somewhere in your heart there is a possibility for us, or else you wouldn't even be here with me now."

"I'm here because my mom insisted."

"All right. That's something. You can't possibly tell me that your family would ever like this guy more than me."

"They do like you a lot, but to be fair, they've never met this other guy."

"That tells me everything I need. If you haven't brought him home, you can't be that serious about him. There's still a chance for us. So tell me, what does he have that I don't have?"

"Why, Allan? So you can try to beat him?"

He put his hand on his chin, like he was striking a thoughtful pose right out of a men's fashion magazine. "I'm interested in working on myself. If he's got some trait that you want, I will try my best to make improvements. Remember how I used to hate girl movies, but I started watching them for you? Like that. So what is it?"

"Well, he's..." Nadine blushed. She could feel her cheeks redden as she spoke. "He's, um, attentive."

"What does that mean? He listens? I listen."

"You do. But not like him. I mean, when I'm with him, it feels like I have his undivided attention at all times. And he's attentive in other ways, too."

"What do you mean?"

She gave him a devious look.

"Oh, now he's better in the sack than me, too?"

"It's not a competition. It's not about better," Nadine said, but her blushing gave her away. "He's just really focused on my pleasure. That's what I mean."

"I'd like the record to state that I've learned a lot since we were together."

"I'm sure."

"Let me prove it to you," he said, taking her hand in his and guiding it to his lips where he kissed it. All the while he stared into her eyes.

Nadine could not ignore the sensations that were building in her. She couldn't fight her animal nature. Her body said yes to Allan instinctively. She found herself appalled by his arrogance intellectually, but turned on simultaneously. How could he manage to have such an effect, she wondered. In her shyness, she picked up her fork and knife and tried to eat again, but it was useless. He had her in his grip.

"I want another date with you to prove to you that I can be attentive."

"Allan, it's not like that. Besides, I'm really busy these days."

"Okay, here's what we're going to do. I'm going to be really observant or whatever and if I can get you to kiss me by the end of the night, then I get to go on another date with you. This Friday night. Do you have plans?"

"Let me check." She took out her phone, which also contained her calendar, and scrolled through her week. She didn't have plans. She wanted to say no out of principle, but she had a weak spot for Allan, especially domineeringly sexy Allan who had the charm turned up fully. "I'm free."

"All right, so it's a plan."

"If I kiss you later, it's a plan," she corrected.

"You will," he said with his typical authority. "You will."

"I'm not letting you come in, by the way."

"Not tonight." He winked. "That's what the second date is for."

Nadine knew she was playing a dangerous game, leading him on like this. It wasn't her style to play games. She avoided them in all other areas of her life. Being up front was more like her. But for some reason, Allan could bring qualities out in her that she hardly recognized. It was as though she was a different person around him.

When the server came to clear the plates and ask whether they wanted dessert, Allan looked at the menu, and ordered passion fruit mousse for the two of them to share. Nadine surprised herself by not interjecting. She wasn't a fan of fruity desserts, especially something as flavorful as passion fruit and particularly after a meal like this. But she let him order anyway and told herself that it was okay to let him take the lead. After all, this was an out of the ordinary experience.

"You really have to come to New York," Allan said. "There are so many places I'd like to show you."

"I've been, you know."

"When?"

"Well, as a kid I went a few times. You knew that."

"Oh, right," Allan said, as though he had suddenly remembered.

"And last year, Marnie and Alfonso and I went for a weekend getaway."

"And you didn't call me?"

"Actually I prayed I wouldn't run into you. I didn't even want to go there. I voted on Montreal. But they insisted. We saw a bunch of sights."

"I could take you places you didn't even know existed. I've seen so much. I feel like the city has really helped me open my mind. Like, for example, there's this little Italian place I like to go to. Luigi, the owner, knows everybody by name. He knows what you like down to whether you take coarse pepper or an extra leaf of basil. The guy is incredible. A real artist."

Nadine couldn't help but think that there were a lot of business owners in Ann Arbor who knew people by name, but somehow Allan had never been impressed.

"Sounds lovely," she said, though she thought it odd to be hearing about a supreme restaurant experience while supposedly having a supreme restaurant experience.

"And of course the music scene…" He told her about places where jazz musicians played to intimate audiences. "Oh, and the arts…" He told her about galleries he went to and a few signed pieces he'd bought for his place, how he wanted a collection of original artwork, how it made him feel good to contribute to the arts as an investor.

When the dessert came, he swiveled his spoon in the light textured mousse and, to Nadine's surprise, he guided the spoon to her lips. This was how they'd shared dessert when they were teenagers. It had been very romantic back then. She opened her mouth, and welcomed the tarty sweet bite. There was an explosion of flavor on her tongue and her mouth began to water. Maybe she wouldn't have chosen this dessert, but it sure was tasty and she was glad to be eating it. She was also aware that in all the years since Allan had spoon-fed her, nobody else had. And it was a particular joy.

* * * *

Nadine got into Allan's BMW after dinner and he waited for her to get her seatbelt on before he closed the door and walked around to the driver's side.

They drove through town and Nadine couldn't help but notice that they weren't far from the furniture shop.

"You know what?" she asked.

"What?"

"My grandpa's old store is up for lease."

"That old place? I'm surprised it's still standing."

"It's a heritage building."

"I'll say. It's seen better days."

"I think it's charming."

"Of course you do. It's called nostalgia."

"I guess so. I still miss Grandpa Winston a lot."

"He was a good guy," Allan said. "Actually, that brings me to the surprise."

They pulled onto Nadine's street and Allan parked in front of the house. He took the keys out of the ignition. It wasn't yet so cold that they needed the heat on.

"Your grandfather called me into his shop after we got engaged."

"He did?"

"Yeah, I guess it was his man-to-man talk, only half of what he said didn't really make sense to me. He used some pretty weird metaphors and stuff. Like he said that love is a journey and there was something about meandering pathways. I mean, what does that mean?"

"I had no idea he talked to you."

"He also gave me something to give to you as a wedding present. He said he knew he probably wouldn't be able to make it to the wedding."

"Yeah, he was already pretty frail by then."

"If you ask me, he shouldn't have been allowed to keep working."

"He didn't consider it work. It was his passion. Besides, it was his home."

"I guess. Anyway, he wanted you to have this." Allan reached to the back seat and pulled a green gift bag to the front. "He said this was a present for you—not for both of us—and that I should give it to you on our wedding day."

"And you had it all this time?"

"I feel terrible I never told you about it, but I kept it safe."

"Oh, Allan." Nadine didn't have a chance to be mad. She was overcome with joy. She was simply filled with emotions—everything from curiosity to sadness to excitement.

She clutched the bag to her. "I don't want to open it here. I'll do it upstairs."

"There were so many times I thought about sending it in the mail or giving it to my parents to give to you, but it never seemed right. I wanted to deliver it myself, and I wanted it to be special. Nadine, I've dated a lot of women since we broke up…"

"Yeah, you made that clear already."

"The point is that none of them were as special as you. You're the marrying kind."

"Hmmm," Nadine said. "I might have changed my views on marriage."

"You? I don't believe it. You had your wedding gown picked out when you were seven years old. Don't you remember how you told me when we were on our first date?"

"Yeah, that was me then. Lately, I haven't felt the same way about it. I like living alone. I like doing my own thing, coming home in the evenings and working on a piece in the garage."

"You're really into this furniture thing, aren't you?"

"Yeah."

"That's cool. I mean, I make a lot of money now. We could afford for you to just do that. And it wouldn't even matter if you sold a lot. You could do it during the day and we could spend the evenings together."

"You've really given this some thought, haven't you?"

"Nadine, what's it going to take? I want you back."

"I need more time to think about it."

"Then kiss me, take a few days and go out with me on Friday."

"Why are you so convincing and confusing at the same time?"

He leaned over the gift bag and came so close that he almost kissed her. They both knew she had to be the one. He closed his eyes. She had to make a choice. Give him another chance — or close a door on him forever.

She kissed him.

* * * *

Once she was alone, she opened the gift bag. Inside, also wrapped in green, there was another package. She cursed Allan for having held onto this for so long. There had been times when she would have given anything for a letter or memento from her grandfather, her kindred spirit.

Gingerly, as though she was touching something that had survived a fire, she slowly peeled back the clear tape from the paper. In her hands, she held a wooden box, about half the size of an average shoebox. She attempted to open it but it was locked. She knew where to find the key, for he had given it to her himself several years before.

All these years, she'd kept the mystery key, a key she had assumed to be ornamental, on the same gold chain that it had come with. In all those years, she'd never imagined that she would one day need it. This was overwhelming and she could not fight back the tears. She felt her grandpa's presence with her now, how he'd always loved surprising her, and it was almost as though he was watching over her as she ran to her bedroom to search through her jewelry box.

The key fit perfectly. She turned it. There was a click. When she opened it, she couldn't believe what she saw.

Chapter Seventeen

Nestled in the box were stacks of hundred dollar bills, more than she'd ever seen before in her life. It was like something out of a drug smuggling or bank heist thriller, and it frightened her so much that she had to close the box for a moment to calm herself down. She looked around as though to make sure that she was alone in her living room. She didn't know what to do with herself. Her hands trembled and she felt her throat go dry.

Opening the lid again, she noticed that, taped to the top of the inside, there was a letter. She took it out and carefully opened the envelope. Crisp browned paper that felt like parchment paper came out. Gently, she unfolded it and started to read.

My dear Nadine,

If you are reading this, you are likely married, so I must begin by offering my congratulations. He's a good man, Allan. Forget what I said about not settling too soon and waiting for the one. I was probably on morphine when I gave you the advice.

As for what you see in this box, I have one single request. You must use this money to follow your heart, even if you want to do something everyone tells you is crazy. It doesn't matter. Life is about the risks we take. Nadine, I have always wanted a life of passion for you. Promise me that you will let yourself follow your dreams with this money.

Your loving granddaddy and kindred spirit,
Winston

Nadine wept. She closed the box with the letter folded back up and placed neatly inside, as though she needed to constrain everything. She held the box in her arms like it was her favorite doll from when she was little. Cradled in her arms, she caressed the smooth wood as the tears flowed. When she held the box to her nose, she could smell that familiar beeswax scent, a combination of orange peel and a hint of spice. It was the scent she associated with his shop and she felt his presence with her in the dark room. She knew she was not alone, that she shared this very moment with her kindred spirit, and she was confident that if he was there with her in person, he would tell her that everything was okay, and so she told herself that it was and tried to believe it. How complicated grieving was. Still now, nearly two years later, she felt a terrible void whenever she craved the guidance that only Grandpa Winston could give.

To comfort herself, Nadine turned to the one soothing experience that never failed to delight. The treat that most reminded her of Grandpa Winston was hot chocolate, so she went to the kitchen, hoping that she had canned milk in the cupboard. She did.

Out came the milk and she opened a different cupboard and found the instant hot chocolate mix, but as soon as she held the circular jar in her hand, she knew it wasn't exactly what she wanted. She'd been forever corrupted by David when it came to hot chocolate. She happened to have a bag of dark chocolate chips from that time her mother came over to bake cookies last Christmas. This was not going to be quite as good as the hot chocolate on the mountain with David, but it'd be a close second and a massive leap from the instant stuff she grew up with.

If only Grandpa Winston could taste this, she thought as she stirred the chocolate chips in a glass bowl on top of a pot of boiling water. She added the melted chocolate to a small saucepan of heated milk and whisked the two together. She was overwhelmed that her grandfather wanted to share his money with her, and how wise he was to tell her to follow her dreams. There were so many clues in the letter to analyze, so much to think about. She wondered about Mrs. Barlow now. It puzzled her that he had wanted her to maintain close contact with her, but it made sense. She had been naïve before. But she began to piece together the hints that begged to coincide with each other in the form of her grandfather's life story. He had married young. Her dad's older sister, Aunt Freda, had been born just six months after the wedding. There had been references to this at family reunions, late at night, after wine.

And she remembered how Grandpa Winston had always admonished against marrying young. To Nadine, her grandfather had seemed to like Allan, but he didn't like the idea of her marrying the first guy she was in love with. He told her so on numerous occasions. *When it's young,* he used to say, *the heart doesn't know what it wants. You have to wait until the heart knows what it wants.*

He was a wise one. That was for sure. The hot chocolate was soothing. She sat at her kitchen table and took sip after careful sip, blowing the steam away gently. The box sat, closed, in front of her. She couldn't count the money. Not yet.

But, as though his spirit had taken her and given her a good shake, she knew exactly what to do with the money.

* * * *

David hadn't heard from Nadine in days and his mind obsessed over the craving he felt to call her. This was not common for him. Girls had a way of coming and going in his life, but this was no girl. Nadine was not only the beautiful goddess of the bookstore, she might very well be his soulmate. His mind raced with thoughts like this and more.

Worse still were the memories that flooded his senses. Sometimes it felt as though he could still taste her on his tongue, like there had been some kind of permanent imprinting that called him back to her, the way he'd once read in a Nigerian poem that those who drank from this particular river in Nigeria would always remember and would always want to return. It had mystified him, when he'd read that poem in some dusty library many years ago. The meaning had eluded him. Now he understood.

He had to rationalize several times a day that she wasn't calling because she was busy, not because she'd forgotten about him. He'd wanted—badly, he realized as he obsessed over each moment—to come across as cool when she visited. Most especially, he had not wanted to come off as jealous. What he had said was true at the time. He was not prone to jealousy. But he had, of course, been speaking about other girls and purely hypothetical situations.

He wasn't possessive. It wasn't in him to want to control her actions and he knew, fundamentally, that he had to give her absolute freedom. Only then would he know that if she returned to him, she really wanted to be with him. He didn't want to put conditions on her. Not now. Not ever. It wasn't the vision he had for the kind of relationship he wanted. He had felt in his heart that they had a connection that transcended the physical. Perhaps he had overshot, driven there by his profound attraction for her, but nevertheless, he refused to call. She must have space, he figured. She had stuff to figure out. Here was this guy who'd come back to town, who wanted to see her, who had a history with her, and she had to come to terms with that. It was not for him to put extra pressure on her.

David stopped himself from dwelling. Instead, he threw himself into his studies. He read Thoreau and tried to imagine himself in a cabin in the woods, but every time he conjured the image, he found himself wondering if Nadine would visit.

He listened to music, but all the lyrics reminded him of Nadine. His roommates even began to suspect.

"Dude," Chris said one night, banging on his door. "What's up with you, man?"

"Nothing, why?"

"You're just in your room all the time is all. You okay?"

"Yeah, fine." David didn't want to get into it. He couldn't explain it. He didn't have the words and he didn't want advice, especially from Chris, who had never even been in love.

"Well, we're watching *Lord of the Rings*. Come out and watch with us. We have pizza."

It was what David needed. Distraction.

But even the movie failed to keep his mind off Nadine, especially Liv Tyler, who bore a striking resemblance to her, now that he looked. There was something equally ethereal and spritely about Nadine, like she wasn't of this world, he thought as they watched the movie in darkness.

He had to let her come back on her own. If there was one thing he didn't want, it was to coerce Nadine into anything. If she wanted him, she'd come back for him. If she didn't, she wouldn't. It was that simple.

And the sooner David got her out of his mind and focused on his other goals, the better. He called up Nick.

"Hey, man, about the hair," he said. "I'm ready."

* * * *

Nadine needed to clear her head. Too much had happened in too short a time. From work, she called up the nursing home where Mrs. Bronstein lived and asked if she could bring Duchess by for a visit. The superintendent said that she'd be most welcome and they scheduled a time for later that afternoon.

Nadine showed up just after four. The sign out front said 'Shady Grove Manor' and the sliding glass doors that opened for her and Duchess seemed welcoming. Everything in the lobby was neat and clean, though there was the unmistakable smell of the elderly. It was a combination of Lily of the Valley, dust and medication. There were residents sitting around in the lobby, half asleep. She asked for Mrs. Bronstein at the front counter.

"Down the hall, to the left," the doorperson said. "Room one-oh-nine."

Nadine could see the excitement in Duchess' wagging tail. She knew. Nadine knocked on the door and waited. After a few minutes she knocked again and heard a faint "Just a minute" from the other side.

The door opened and a little lady yelled out, "Duchess!"

Duchess entered immediately and the woman bent down to rub the dog on the top of her head. Duchess panted and whimpered.

Mrs. Bronstein was a frail-looking stylish woman with a colorful turban and a kimono. "Come in," she said.

Her room was reminiscent of the seventies with orange dome lamps and psychedelic paintings on the wall. She even had a beaded curtain that she hobbled through. Nadine followed her.

"Thank you for bringing my Duchess for a visit. You are an angel. Please, sit down."

She gestured to an orange vinyl sofa. Nadine tried not to overreact to the funky retro look of the place, but she couldn't help but look around in fascination.

"Duchess is such a great dog," she said. "I'm sorry you couldn't bring her with you."

Mrs. Bronstein shook her head. "You get to be my age and it's too much work. I'm glad she's got a good home — and Duke, too."

"Duke found a home?" Nadine's heart practically leapt out of her chest at the news.

"Yes. A young gentleman took him. A real saint, he is. You know, Duke had some health problems." She rubbed her finger and forefinger together to suggest the counting of money. "It wasn't going to be cheap for the new owner and honestly, I didn't think he'd make it. I'm just overjoyed. He's doing fine, though. Came to see me yesterday afternoon. Such a fine young man."

"Wow, that's so nice. I can't tell you how happy I am to hear it," Nadine said. "If I were in a different position financially, I'd have taken both. I mean, they're a real pair."

"That they are. Never separated, you know."

"So I heard."

"Well, dear, tell me about yourself." She got comfortable in her sitting chair. "Would you like a cup of tea? You'll have to make it, but it's the good stuff. I got it at a tea shop. And I have cookies, too."

This was exactly what Nadine needed—a little maternal guidance from a woman who had a bong on her shelf, right next to her collection of Gloria Steinem and Alice Walker books.

"Yes, please. I'll put on the kettle."

Nadine filled the small kettle in the washroom by using the tea cup as a scoop for the water. Mrs. Bronstein did indeed have an elaborate tea collection, including a slotted spoon in which to lay loose leaf tea. She was either a connoisseur herself or her children were.

"This is a lovely selection of tea paraphernalia, Mrs. Bronstein," Nadine remarked.

"Oh, thank you. It's from my beau."

"Oh?"

"Yes. Mr. Delacroix. He lives here, too. In the other wing."

"Really?" Nadine was surprised for some reason, though she caught herself before she made too much of it. "How nice." She didn't want to pry.

"Yes. He came calling a few months ago."

"Oh, so it's a new relationship?" Nadine smiled to herself. This was exactly the kind of distraction she needed.

"Yes, and I'm afraid I'll be letting him down easy pretty soon."

"That's too bad. Any reason?"

"He's too old for me, dear. Too old-fashioned."

"What do you mean?"

"I mean he had a different type of life than I did — a wife who stayed at home and tended the children and all that. I have had a — shall we say — unconventional life. Never married. One kid, adopted. Cheryl is her name. She's a singer."

"But you call yourself *Mrs.*" Nadine pointed out, wanting to hear why before Mrs. Bronstein moved on. She seemed like the kind of woman who could gloss right over the most important stuff.

She shrugged. "That's what they call me around here."

"Even though you were never a Mrs.?"

"It's a generational thing. Most women in my generation go by Mrs. It's a silly little thing and I don't give a hoot one way or another, so I just let them call me whatever they want. As long as they call, I say." She laughed at her own joke.

Nadine laughed, too. She couldn't believe the story on many levels — both the strange assumptions people make and Mrs. Bronstein's blatant disregard.

"Wow. So your daughter's a singer?"

"Oh yes. She also plays bass guitar. She's touring right now with a band, all throughout the southern states. They have a big gig coming up in Nashville in a couple of weeks."

"Whoa. That's amazing. How old is your daughter?"

"Oh, she's what now? Fifty-three."

"And touring? That's very cool." Her own mother was around that age, but somehow it was impossible to conjure an image of her mom getting her groove on in a band.

"She has some CDs out. Maybe you've heard of them. The Molly Miller Band?"

"Sounds familiar."

"They play on the radio from time to time. She makes a living. Don't get me wrong, it's not an easy life. But she followed her heart and that's what matters."

The tea was ready to steep in the teapot. Nadine placed it on a trivet on the coffee table. She told Mrs. Bronstein—Stella—about the Allan situation and how it had interrupted a budding romance with a young guy she'd met at work.

"The thing is, it seems so tempting to go back to Allan. I loved him so much and was devastated when he left. Our families love each other. That's important. And he wants to take care of me."

"I hear two red flags in what you just said. One, you said love in the past tense. Two, when men promise to take care of you, there are strings attached."

Nadine thought about it. She could never admit this to her own mother or Jeraldine Jordan, of course, but Allan's vision did sit funny with her. "He said I could work on my furniture business from home during the day, and it wouldn't matter if it became a commercial success or not."

"Ouch."

"Yeah, I mean, I get it. He wants me to follow my heart and be happy in doing the work that I love, but..."

"He doesn't understand that you're a serious businesswoman."

"I think he thinks what everyone in our families thinks, too, that one day I'll just make the same choice I grew up with and stay home and raise kids. The truth is, I'm not even sure I want them."

"How old are you?"

"Thirty-two."

"Oh, honey. There's lots of time for children and they don't have to come from your body in order to be your kids. Believe me."

"I do." Nadine sighed. "Thanks for talking with me, Stella. Sometimes I feel like nobody understands."

"What about Allan? Do you feel like he understands you?"

Nadine thought about it and her eyes became teary. "I don't."

"Then you'd better let him go."

"Even though on paper we're perfect?"

"What does that mean?"

"It means if you write down everything about us on a piece of paper, we match perfectly."

"Who cares about paper? You need a guy who understands you. Otherwise, you're better off alone. There's nothing wrong with that, you know. You get to choose who comes and goes. It's a sweet life. How long has it been since you had sex?"

Nadine wondered if it was written all over her. "I had a pretty great experience not too long ago. Why do you ask?"

"Duke's new dad. He's very handsome, and he's one of the good ones. I can tell."

"No thanks." Nadine shook her head. "I've got enough going on. The guy who gave me that incredible experience I just mentioned? That wasn't Allan."

"Oh?"

"Yeah. See, there's this other guy. And on paper we're *so* not perfect. He's over a decade younger than me."

"Sounds delightful. If only Mr. Delacroix were about ten years younger."

"You don't think it matters?"

"I think there are a lot of other things that matter more. Tell me, do you feel like this younger guy understands you?"

Nadine didn't need to think about it. She nodded.

"So there you go."

"But I'm not sure I want to be with him."

"Because?"

"We're different."

"Difference is good," Mrs. Bronstein said.

"That's what he said."

"He's smart."

* * * *

Nadine got into her work overalls. All the drama of her romantic life had taken its toll on her ability to focus on the one thing that really mattered – her business. She turned on the light in the garage and plugged in the tiny space heater for the first time this year. It was too brisk to be outside in the garage without a little extra heat.

She got out her sanding equipment. It was time to strip the pale yellow paint off an old country table. This was the kind of thing she could really sink herself into. There was nothing like starting a new project, seeing what was beneath the surface and bringing it to light.

She took a break and looked around her garage, which functioned as a tool shed. On the wall, there was a framed picture of her and Grandpa Winston at his shop. She must have been twelve or thirteen. She put down the sander and walked over to the picture and studied it. Who was that girl who had wanted to get married so badly? She barely recognized her. A ghost from the past, she was now.

The past couple of years had changed her. Allan's leaving then her job no longer needing her and giving her the ax like that... Then losing the most important mentor of her life. All so abrupt. She knew one thing. Her grandfather was right. Life has no guarantees and you can't control other people or their actions, nor should you try. Things either worked out or they didn't. It shouldn't be hard. And you should never spend time with someone who doesn't fully accept you, nor should you ever try to change anyone. People are as they are, she thought, as she surveyed the garage and felt her heart swell with pride that she had — against her ex-fiancé's advice — followed this dream. She loved furniture and working with wood and helping people create the homes they wanted. All of it was beautiful to her, especially the many, many hours she'd get to spend by herself lost in thought.

She went back to work. That was it. As she sanded away at the table, she knew what her heart desired more than anything else.

Reaching for her cell phone, she dialed the number.

"Hi, Jack? It's Nadine." She felt her grandpa's presence with her in the austere garage. "I'd like to lease the shop."

* * * *

Friday night came around and Nadine wanted to be ready for seven, as she and Allan had agreed. She got dressed and did her hair and makeup, but everything was off. Her stomach was in knots. She didn't want this date. She had agreed to it because of a stupid trick, Allan's annoying kissing game. Even with the stakes as high as they were for her, Allan couldn't help but turn everything into some sort of betting game.

Did she want a man like this?

What about everything she'd divulged to Stella? It had seemed pretty clear then that she didn't want Allan. So why was she going through these motions? She owed him nothing. Less than nothing.

By the time Allan knocked on the door, Nadine had loosened herself up with two glasses of chardonnay.

"Come on up," she said, ignoring the flowers he held.

"These are for you," he said.

"Okay. Bring them up," she said with her back to him. She was already halfway up the steps.

"How was your week? Were you looking forward to seeing me?"

"My week was —" She paused, searching for the right word. She settled on — "*Illuminating.*"

"Cool. I don't know what that means, but you look great."

"Thanks," she said through pursed lips.

He went through her cupboards, the very ones he had once shared with her. He knew where to find a vase, and he wasted no time in filling one with water. He cut open the bouquet paper and snipped off the bottoms of the stems, then sprinkled some of the powder from the florist into the water.

"Have you given any thought to us?" Allan asked.

"I have. It's not going to work."

"Just like that?"

"Well, it's not like it's some kind of impromptu decision, Allan. I've given it a lot of thought."

"I'll be more attentive, I swear."

"It's not that. There's nothing you can do."

"But, Nadine. We're perfect. Everyone knows that. I'm sorry it took me too long to figure it out. I'm sorry about the mistakes I made, but you can't change the past."

"I don't want to restore furniture as a hobby, while I pop out kids and support you in your career."

"Who said anything about that? We could get you a store, if you prefer."

"That. Right there. That idea is so condescending, Allan. At the end of the day, you want me to be your dependent. You'll give me the illusion that I'm doing something empowering and independent, but really, you will be the one footing the bills."

"Well, come on, Nadine. Do you really believe you'll be able to support yourself on restoring furniture in this economy? People want new stuff. Nobody gives a crap about antiques anymore."

There it was.

One sentence that told her everything she needed to know.

Nadine stood, shocked into silence, and stared at the man she had once loved.

"Goodbye, Allan."

"That's it? No dinner? No nothing? I made reservations."

"So go on your own if it's that important to you."

"Whoa. Where's all this anger coming from? I've never seen you like this."

"That's just it, Allan. You've never seen me."

Chapter Eighteen

That weekend, Nadine Baxter dressed in her Alfred Sung dress. She put her hair in a sensible bun and applied a little makeup, but not too much. It was important that she look like the kind of woman who could run a furniture restoration shop to whomever this landlord was she was about to meet. She wanted to make a good impression, and she didn't think her work overalls would cut it, though she couldn't wait to have days in the shop where she tended to customers in her work clothes, just like Grandpa Winston did.

Before she left for the meeting, she checked herself out in the full-length mirror. Something was missing and she saw precisely what it was. She went to her jewelry box and got out the necklace with the key on it. Yes, she thought as she put it on, this was their day together. He was with her. She knew it and felt it deeply in her heart. Now she was ready.

She and Duchess got into the car and pulled out of the driveway. As she drove past David's neighborhood, she realized that she missed him. But no mind, she thought. She couldn't afford to distract herself from her vision—not over a man. Men were fleeting and made promises they didn't keep. There was no reason to torture herself over something that wouldn't work out anyway. They were in different places in their lives. It was best to focus on what was tangible. Furniture. Duchess. The shop. She fantasized about making a replica of the original sign that Grandpa Winston had made himself. Nothing would please her more than returning the shop to its halcyon days, name included—*Winston's Fine Furniture. Established 1965.*

Her heart beat hard in her chest, and she tried to breathe deeply. This was it. She was going to sign her name to this, give up her safe job at the bookstore and make a real go of it. Even a month ago, she hadn't been ready, but somehow the events of the past few weeks had taught her that she wasn't as reliant on security and safety as she had thought. She was ready to take a risk, ready to follow her dream. With her grandpa's money, she was going to do something that might look stupid to everyone she knew, but this was something she would never regret, not ever.

She parked the car, rolled down the window for Duchess and told her to stay in the car and that they'd go to the park right after the meeting. One last deep breath and a quick lipstick check in the rearview mirror and she got out, briefcase in hand.

Jack Harrington greeted her at the door.

"You're early," he said. "The landlord will be here in fifteen or so. Why don't I show you around?"

"Sure. Can I ask you something? Is there still an apartment attached to the shop?"

"Yeah, it's kind of small, so I just use it for overstock. Come with me."

He turned on his heels and walked toward the familiar old door that connected the shop to the outside corridor. He unlocked the door and pushed it open. The stairs leading up to the second floor still creaked like Nadine remembered.

He unlocked the second door to the apartment and gestured for her to go inside. She was overwhelmed by the familiarity of it. The sun through the window cast its glow and though the place was full of boxes and bins that weren't there when she knew it, there were a surprising amount of items still left from her Grandpa's time, including the old clock on the wall and the kettle on the old gas stove.

"Go ahead and look around," Jack said. "Don't mind the mess. I can have it out of here by the end of the month if everything goes ahead today."

"Thanks." Nadine went to the bay window first. How many memories did she have of daydreaming while gazing out of these windows? It was such a beautiful view of the old neighborhood and the park just behind. The leaves were still on the trees and they shone their various hues of orange, yellow and brown in the afternoon sun. This was the world as she wanted to see it. She was home.

When she turned back around, she noticed a rounded wooden corner sticking out from behind a pile of boxes. Could it be?

She ran to it and pulled on the corner to discover that yes, in fact, it was. Her grandfather's sign was still there, perfectly intact. It was ready to hang outside again. Nadine tried to fight the tears, thinking it inappropriate to bring her sentimentality to a business meeting, but she couldn't help herself. She was ecstatic that the sign had been perfectly preserved all these years.

"I think I hear him down there," Jack said. "Let's get this meeting over with. I for one can't wait to sign on the dotted line."

"Yeah, let's go," Nadine said, closing the apartment door behind her.

They walked down the steps and she followed Jack into the shop. She stepped into the shop and got the shock of a lifetime.

She did a double take. It couldn't be. This guy had short hair and he was wearing a suit. He looked like he'd stepped out of a *GQ* photo shoot. This was definitely not the rugged, long-haired guy she'd gone on a date with.

"David?"

"Nadine." He offered her a handshake.

"What are you doing here?"

"Well—" He cleared his throat. "If you're here to lease the shop, then I should probably introduce myself as your new landlord."

Nadine folded her hands across her chest.

"Can I talk to you?" Her voice was stern.

"Sure," David said. He stood still, waiting for her to begin talking.

"Outside."

"Okay." He followed her out onto the sidewalk where the air was chilly. He examined her face. She looked vexed. "Is something the matter?"

"Yeah," she scoffed. "You lied."

"What? No. Never."

"You did. At the very least, you misrepresented. All your talk of philosophy and living on the beach. What the hell was all that? You own buildings?"

"Building. Singular."

"But how? Why?"

"I told you I'd made some investments. I told you I designed that little app that made a few bucks."

"I thought that you meant it literally."

"That's the operative part of your statement—*you thought*." He remained cool and collected. "My parents also left some insurance money."

"But you slept in your car for a year. You have roommates."

"So? I'm a minimalist."

"Then what's with the suit?"

"It's the only one I own. A man's gotta have one suit. Even Thoreau thinks so."

She shook her head in disbelief. Boy did she not enjoy being wrong about people. But she had to admit it. He hadn't lied. She had filled in the details of what he'd said with false information based on her own prejudices.

"Well, look. I don't know what to make of this. I was so sure that I'd be signing the dotted line today, but now I have to think about it."

"Why? It's your dream."

"Yeah, well, I didn't know you'd be a part of it."

She turned on her heels and walked away.

* * * *

When she had finished her work on Wednesday afternoon, Nadine went to the washroom and changed into her running gear. When she came back into the Shipping and Receiving area, she was wearing her track pants and a zippered tight-fitting running top. Everything matched. It was all white. She even had a matching white headband that went around her ears to protect her from the cooler temperatures.

Duchess was excited by the change of clothes. Nadine put all of her usual business attire into her backpack, pulled it over her shoulder and locked the door to her department. It was foggy out and there was that faint fall glow of white in the air.

With Duchess at her side, she started off through the campus, slowly at first. It was a thirty-minute run home and she was looking forward to cutting through the park where the leaves were falling, as the sun was beginning to make its descent. The shadows this time of year were magical and ethereal. Besides, she needed to work off some of the angst that had built inside her since everything had gotten even more messy and confusing.

In the park, Duchess took off for the first time ever. This was so uncharacteristic that Nadine knew it must mean she was chasing after something. They were a hunting breed after all. Maybe she'd spotted a rabbit or squirrel. But even as she veered off the path, following her dog down a side path, she knew that they'd encountered plenty of small animals before and Duchess had never bolted. She was so well behaved.

Through the fog, up ahead, she saw Duchess take off even faster, so fast that she was out of sight entirely.

Then, through the falling leaves, she saw something that appeared to be a vision out of a dream. It was Duchess playing with Duke. Could it be that she was imagining this? Nadine ran to them and that's when she saw David running toward the dogs from a different part of the park. The dogs were like Catherine and Heathcliff running toward each other, and now they were playing and prancing and jumping on each other.

"What?" Nadine was incredulous. "You mean?"

David nodded. "I adopted Duke."

"Oh my God. Mrs. Bronstein—Stella—said Duke was adopted by a handsome young man."

David looked bashful for a moment. "I just came from visiting her."

"Whoa," Nadine said, finding it nearly impossible to take in the fact that Stella had wanted to set her up with David, that David had cut his hair, that David owned the building she wanted to lease. All of it was just too weird. She turned her attention to Duke instead. He looked well. His wagging tail told her everything.

She crouched down, but Duke took no notice of her. He was off frolicking with Duchess. "How're you doing, boy?"

"He had the operation a couple of weeks ago. The vet said the tumors were benign, so he's going to be okay." He got down on one knee and called Duke to him and said, "Aren't you, boy? You're going to be just fine."

"I can't believe this," Nadine said. "Duchess has never taken off before."

"Yeah, they're drawn to each other," David said. "They used to be inseparable."

Nadine knew he was insinuating something about the two of them, but she didn't want to give in.

"I feel like I don't know who you are," she said. "You presented yourself one way, then showed me something else entirely. It's hard to trust that."

"I never lied to you."

"You also never told me that you bought my grandfather's building. I'd call that a pretty big omission."

"I should have mentioned it."

"I'll say," she huffed.

"All my life, I've wanted to be seen for me, not for my circumstances. When I lost my family, everyone looked at me with pity. I hated it. When I inherited my parents' savings, I could tell that those same people who had looked at me like I was a lost and wounded puppy dog started to look at me like I was some kind of spoiled trust fund kid. That pissed me off even more. I guess that's when I started to get secretive. I knew when I started studying at UMich that I did not want my friends and roommates to know that I'd already made my first million. I guess I'm just sick of people treating me differently. I promised myself a year of just concentrating on philosophy without any other complications. So, no, I didn't mean to lie to you, but I also didn't want to tell the whole truth because I felt I owed myself."

Nadine listened. David's intensity was too much for her sometimes. He was no boy toy, nor was he immature. He knew himself and the world better than anyone she'd ever met. She was transfixed by him. And just like the epiphany that had hit so hard a little over a year ago when she knew in her heart that she had to restore furniture, in this moment she knew that she loved David.

"David..."

"The furniture shop is yours, all right? It was always yours. I happen to hold the title to the building, but so what? Don't let that stand in the way of your dream. You don't even have to talk to me, unless you have some kind of plumbing issue I need to handle."

"David..."

"And I know you know I'm not fond of your fiancé, but business is business. If you want to be with him, I'm not standing in your way."

"I..."

"And as for these two," he said, looking at Duke and Duchess frolicking around each other, "well, they won't understand why they've been separated, but they'll live."

"David. Shut up."

Nadine's command worked. David stopped talking. He looked at her with those warm eyes of his, and she knew what to do.

Nadine went to him. She put her arms around him. He held her tight and in his arms she knew she had found the one.

Epilogue

Nadine watched David haul the last of her boxes up the creaky steps to her tiny new apartment above Grandpa Winston's shop. She smiled, thinking about the crazy way life works out.

When the kettle boiled, Nadine announced that it was officially break time for the entire crew that was helping her move — David, Marnie and Nick.

"Beer or tea?" Nadine asked her friends.

"Beer," Marnie said.

Nick smiled at her. "Now that's my kind of woman."

Nadine passed drinks around. She opened a bag of organic jerky and took out two pieces for Duke and Duchess. The pair sat down next to each other in front of her. She laughed at them, an unlikely coupling, but perfect in their own way. Maybe perfect on paper wasn't all she'd believed it to be.

She was home.

About the Author

Romance heroines have saved my sanity numerous times through break-ups and life changes. I find escaping into a romance both soothing and revitalizing—and even better when there are some steamy scenes to tantalize the imagination.

For most of my adult life, I've concentrated on carving out a serious career, but a number of love-hungry, sassy characters keep taking over my mind, insisting that I daydream, live vicariously through them and tell their stories. Watching these women emerge on the page gives me a different sort of satisfaction than I get from my day job. It is a joy to share them with readers.

I live in a tiny apartment in a crowded city and I like to think there is something romantic about this. I did manage to find my soul mate here.

Destiny Moon loves to hear from readers. You can find her contact information, website details and author profile page at http://www.totallybound.com.

Home of Erotic Romance